BOOKS BY EIZABETH COOKE

Life Savors – A Memoir
Eye of the Beholder
A Shadow Romance
There's a Small Hotel,
(Winner Paris Book Festival 2015 for General Fiction)
Secrets of a Small Hotel
The Hotel Next Door
A Tale of Two Hotels
Rendezvous at a Small Hotel,
(Grand Prize Winner Paris Book Festival 2016)
The Hotel Marcel Dining Club – By Invitation Only
How To Game People Without Even Trying
Still Life – A Love Story
The Rose Trilogy
Violet Rose – The Encroaching Sea
Starfish – The Arbitrary Ocean
Violet – The Swelling Tide
Abbi's Forever Home
Abbi's Forever Home – FOR KIDS

www.elizabethcookebooks.com

Author's Rep: marciagrosen@gmail.com

Shadow Box

Elizabeth Cooke

Abbott Press books may be ordered through booksellers or by contacting:

Abbott Press
1663 Liberty Drive
Bloomington, IN 47403
www.abbottpress.com
Phone: 1 (866) 697-5310

Cover art by Todd Engel Creative.

ISBN: 978-1-4582-2259-6 (sc)
ISBN: 978-1-4582-2258-9 (hc)
ISBN: 978-1-4582-2257-2 (e)

Library of Congress Control Number: 2019919590

Print information available on the last page.

Abbott Press rev. date: 11/26/2019

INTRODUCTION

A shadow box is an enclosing case behind a glass pane displaying something important and in need of protection. Often, in life, a woman is confined behind the glass.

The shadow box of sexual play – shadowed – boxed in – hot. There is provocation – often harassment – innuendo and deceit. There are sexual escapades without actual intercourse. There is flirtation and date rape and horny sailors, who on arriving in New York Harbor on great ships at the end of World War 11, inflated condoms and sent them into the air like tiny balloons.

There is the ballad from Otis Redding from that time, in the 40s, entitled "Try a Little Tenderness" that proclaims, "Love is her whole happiness. Try a little tenderness." Hah! Love is her WHOLE happiness?

Today, there is not only the glass ceiling of power to shatter, but the box of glass – of life's confinement of women, starting way back in a more primitive world, in the stable where the human female lived, and was considered property like one of the cows or camels.

Later, as time went on, there was the box of marriage, childrearing, the box of home, of abuse, of the marital bed – on demand – with or without desire, the box of conventional expectations, the box of the judgment of her peers. For poorer women, it was worse. Today, the 21st century provides a different dynamic: the shadow box of sexual submission shattered.

THIS IS NOW

MARCIE- 2019

Samantha and her granddaughter, Marcie, were having a pasta dinner at the round glass table at the end of Sammy's living room. At 25, young and beautiful, Marcie, who lived in Los Angeles, was visiting her beloved relative in Atlanta for a couple of weeks, early in the spring. She adored her grandmother. The two were always very frank together.

"How's your love life?" Samantha asked with a smile, as she spread more Parmesan over her spaghetti. Marcie didn't answer.

"Where and how does one meet potential 'friends' these days?" the older woman persisted.

"Through fate – but not at an event everyone's enthused about," said Marcie.

"Do you desire an old fashioned family?"

"No, but I do want a baby." She paused. "Yet the planet is so scary to bring the poor little thing into."

The two continued to devour the delicious dish in its red sauce with juicy meatballs.

Marcie put her fork down. "There are new types of togetherness today– not like in your day, Grandma. Don't mean to offend…"

Samantha started to laugh. "Sweetheart, you couldn't offend me."

"Today… as partners, we would each want our own space – maybe a bridge between…like Diego Rivera had with his mistress. Oh, I'm not against marriage, but the fantasy about it is gone. I want integrity, loyalty. I don't want to be put in some sort of box."

"Hmm…a box?" Samantha continued, "You used the word 'partner'… male or female?"

"Doesn't matter. I want character, someone supportive of my work, honest, humorous, creative, has to be attractive. It's icy water for me right now- not undeserved – my reaction to men making themselves into victims has been pretty strong. They seem to feel emasculated – with a weird resentment at not being in control and no longer entitled. Heck, men call harassment suits 'witch hunts'! That word 'WITCH'…says a lot about them."

"Tell me," Samantha said, as she poured each of them more Cabernet Sauvignon. "What do you find romantic? Romance was so much a part of the love game as I grew up."

Marcie paused. Then, "Romantic? I guess certain songs. There is one by James Blake with the lyric 'I'll come too'. He needs to follow her. 'I can go there too. Can't believe the way we flow.' You know…"

Samantha laughed again. "No I don't."

"I'm fluid about sex," her granddaughter said laconically as she buttered her dinner roll.

"What does that mean, Marcie?"

"Well, gender just doesn't matter. Who you're attracted to…"

"Bisexual?" Sammy asked gently.

"No. More."

"More?"

"Transgender people – genderless people, the androgynous ones – people into fetishes, even kinky stuff."

"Huh?" Samantha was nonplussed.

"They exist." There was a pause. "It just matters who you're attracted to – who you want to be with – physically – who supports you and your dreams…"

"I'm confused." And Samantha was.

"It could be anyone. That's what's so exciting."

"It could be any one - or any thing."

"Any thing?"

"Why yes," Samantha said. "In the really olden days, a shepherd might use his goat or his cow…"

"Oh Grandma, Come on!"

"It's true." They continued with the wine.

"Pansexual is not like that."

"Pansexual? That's a new word for me. Now I'm really confused. God, I'm 93 years old. It's not only a new 'word' but a new world altogether."

Marcie laughed and looked at Samantha. "You're younger than you think." And she lifted her glass. "To you, Grandma. Here's to you."

Their two glasses clicked. Then, Samantha posed what to her was a loaded question. "What's it like? Pansexuality?"

Her granddaughter made a little face and said softly, "I don't exactly know. I guess I'll know when I see him or her..."

"Or it," Samantha couldn't resist saying, as Marcie threw back her head and laughed.

Samantha joined her. Then, "Tell me, darling. With all the world to choose from, it makes it almost irresistible to cheat, I mean, doesn't it?"

"Well, if you are with your soul partner, it wouldn't happen," Marcie responded primly.

"In the old days, when a woman married, she kept her earlier men friends at a distance...in deference to her husband in a way. As a married couple, they socialized with other couples."

"How boring."

"Maybe that's what I mean," Samantha persisted. "As a pansexual, temptation is everywhere. There are no boundaries."

"Except the boundaries of love," Marcie remarked, which to Samantha was an oxymoron.

Helping herself at the stove to more spaghetti and sauce, Marcie called across to the dining table. "Then of course, there's polyamory!"

"What? Polyamory? Many amours – at once?"

"Hey, you get it, Grandma," the younger woman said, sitting down again at the table with her heaping plate. "It has been described as 'consensual, ethical, and responsible non-monogamy'."

"Non-monogamy?" Samantha shook her head.

"Well, couples living together."

"By couples, you mean more than one couple."

"Yes. Perhaps several – some live in a group and- you know- share their partners, I guess."

"No one gets jealous?" Samantha couldn't help smiling. "Even a little bit…"

"Sex has nothing to do with a deep committed long term loving relationship for the polyamory person."

"Yeah, sure!" said her grandmother, with another shake of her head, dismissing the intrusive images of group sex. "And all the partners are consenting?"

"Right. No one gets hurt. They all are mighty satisfied…I guess…"

Guess again, Samantha thought. How thankful she was to have lived in the 20th century, not the 21st – even though polyamorous people must have existed for a long time. Her ignorance of it had been a gift.

Until now.

FOOD

"I wonder if the lure of food entices a polyamorous person," Samantha murmured to herself as she cleared the table. Marcie had retired to the guest bedroom to sleep off her jet lag.

"Does delectable food still whet the sexual appetite?" Samantha wondered to herself. "It sure used to," she said aloud. "Lobster dripping in butter, a perfect sweet melon with slices of salty prosciutto, caviar with lemon on a buckwheat blini – maybe with a dollop of *crème fraiche*...ah such sweet dreams of a kind of foreplay."

Samantha was busy washing the dinner dishes in the kitchen sink. She continued to brood. Or does this day of digital devices and on-line dating curb and tamp down the natural flow between one appetite and the next? And as for the polyamorous ones, what a way to live! "Do they bother to eat?" this said aloud.

What they are missing! How sensual it is, the sexiness of delicious food, and how anticipatory, she thought. A warm apple pie... a warm bed. A spicy pizza... a hot bed. Whipped cream... Well, that was classic and beyond imagination.

"Do these two carnal senses still match? It's hard to believe they do in this age of hook-up bars, hook-up texts, in a hook-up world, where non-monogamy is a way of life, at least for some."

"Listen to me," Samantha said in a loud voice. "The lazy, sexy, hazy dream seems long ago."

She turned off the water in the sink, shut off the light and left the kitchen, her voice low, softly saying "so sad," and as she brushed her hair, preparing for a night of rest, she remembered *Pierre,* a French doctor in Paris, and the dinner she had prepared for him…for them… the two *amants.*

What a memory. Samantha had lived for a year in Paris, after her divorce from first husband, Joseph. It was 1960.

Her charming (married) French/English doctor was coming to her apartment at *Onze, rue Monsieur* for a dinner prepared in Sam's best *Cordon Bleu* manner. She had not attended the prestigious cooking school for no reason. A six weeks course – 9:00 to 5:00 – five days a week – with a chef with a wooden leg who looked like Santa Claus – who had drilled into her – an eager culinary pupil – certain facts of *haute cuisine!*

And she planned to put them to good use to seduce her soon- to-be lover.

"Food can be so sexy," she muttered to herself as she remembered deciding on the menu for *Pierre.* "First, tiny blini with *crème fraiche* and salmon roe, the bright red caviar, as garnish. Then, *paupiettes de veau,* thin veal cutlets stuffed with a savory pork mixture, browned in butter, in that elegant sauce with white wine and *tomate concentré.*" Samantha was beginning to salivate.

"So delicious," she breathed.

"Then, of course, a small butter lettuce salad with just lemon and oil dressing – and a good *Pont* L'Évêque cheese – and *finalement,* hmm… something refreshing – something sweet…hmmm. Aha! *Oranges à la Cyrano.* Perfect. I can make them ahead – first hollow out the oranges, mix their juice with whipped cream and gelatin, stuff and put in the refrigerator with a cherry on top."

She realized this would take all day to create – but it would be so worth it. Her *Docteur Pierre* would delight in every sumptuous morsel, dripping with the juices of love.

And, of course, there had been the large, soft bed in the adjoining room at *Onze, rue Monsieur,* where perhaps…with maybe more whipped cream, she thought, every sensory organ awaiting expectantly. Ah yes.

But, back to reality. As Samantha lay in her bed in Atlanta, she smiled and whispered to herself, "Ah, yes. I remember it well."

IS FLIRTATION DEAD?

It is June 6th, 2019, the 75th anniversary of D-Day. The poignant memories flowed over and through Samantha, as she lay on her bed in Atlanta. Her precious granddaughter (actually step-granddaughter – although the two of them were as tight as blood could have made them), was nearby, oblivious. Marcie slept soundly in the next room, as the invasion of the Normandy beach so long ago loomed brilliant in Samantha's mind.

Samantha's thoughts shifted. Here and now, in the quietude of her own bedroom, she envisioned, as from a distance, the changing mores of her countrymen – and in fact the world – in terms of the shadow box of sex.

How women have changed, she thought; men too, of course. How men and women lose gender identity as they age – often with families gyrating to gay lovers later in life or bisexuality. Perhaps that has gone on forever.

But the matchmaking apps on the internet: the bars – particularly in large urban areas that provide instant pickups – across a crowded room – followed by immediate consummation: the self-promoting celebrities who appear half naked (or fully so) to show off toned and plastic sculpted bodies: the enormous attention to sexual harassment in the workplace – theater, factory, office, restaurant – where dominant men find the power imbalance between male and female so intensely erotic... "What a world," she said aloud.

"And pansexuality and polyamory! I guess it's been around

forever – but somehow is more visible now. Such a puzzlement!" she exclaimed to herself, over and over.

It was far from Samantha's early world and life. She had modified the definition of the shadow box in her mind. She now believed – particularly in terms of predatory advances – that a woman boxing with an imaginary opponent, found suddenly that foe had become visible and dangerous and very, very real.

Flirtation today is dead. The fun of a wink, a compliment, a personal remark –"That blue sweater's beautiful. It matches your eyes" – verboten! The construction worker's whistle on the street, as a pretty woman passes by - unacceptable! A casual touch, a hug, even an air-kiss, or the natural male hand under a woman's elbow to help her into a car or escort her into a dining room – no more!

"It's all changed, the game of love," Samantha said softly, as she drifted off. She had read a recent article in the newspaper where people were outraged and offended by the song from the 1940s: "Baby, It's Cold Outside."

The song is the story of a woman who wants to spend the night and is looking for excuses to stay. Are we at a point where human warmth and romance are illegal, Samantha asked herself? It was written as World War 11 was upending norms: women were in the work force and even in the armed services, so traditional courtships were disturbed. The song depicts a man and woman's sexual desire in a most playful way.

Samantha started to laugh. Taking issue with a song from so long ago that was nothing more than a flirtatious exchange between a man and a woman obviously attracted to one another was ridiculous. The protests against the lyrics, so harsh and outrageous, showed a societal disconnect that was crazy.

With that in mind, Samantha finally fell asleep.

A LAST BREAKFAST

As Marcie stayed with Samantha for almost two weeks, her grandmother noticed how often she was glancing at her phone – "it's really a little computer now, Grandma" – and sitting absorbed in her laptop. Samantha found it bothersome.

Marcie was to be picked up by an Uber driver to take her to the airport at 8:30 AM. As Samantha prepared what was to be their final meal together of this trip, thoughts of love today and those of yesteryear plagued the older woman.

It was near 7:00 when Marcie emerged from the guest bedroom. Samantha started to whip up the eggs. Bacon was already simmering in the oven.

"How'd you sleep?"

"Okay, I guess. I'm always restless before a flight."

"I remember," Samantha said, sliding two English muffins into the toaster. "Here, darling..." and she handed Marcie a cup of black coffee, to which she replied, "Thanks. I need this. At least I'm all packed," and slowly sank to her seat at the table.

There was silence as Samantha completed the two plates, buttered the muffins and brought the food over to be enjoyed.

"Mmm. Mmm," Marcie said. "Smells so good."

"Well, dig in." And both did.

"You know, I've been thinking about some of our conversations."

"Which one?" Marcie asked, laughing. "We've had quite a few during these days together."

"Well, the particular conversations about love."

"It bothers you... that I am ...what? ... more open to possibilities than was true in your time?"

"No really. It's just that I noticed you are up late, on your Skype screen communicating with someone..."

"Yes. It's a fellow I met once at an Internet conference. We text and phone and talk on Skype all the time. It's amazing how much you can learn about a person, and it is really intimate in a way. It's almost like he's sitting next to me on the bed. Skype is so clear... it makes him seem right there."

Samantha grinned. "Clear, huh... But it doesn't sound all that intimate to me."

"Maybe," Marcie grinned back, "but remember, with one click, he's gone."

Samantha took a bite of muffin, then "You want this type of safe, sanitized... what... relationship?"

"No, but Skype... His face is so real and his expressions. It's like there's no distance."

"So you've met this Mr. Skype?"

"That one time, but we plan to get together soon."

Samantha rose and took the plates to the sink in the kitchen. "More coffee?" she called. "Oh please," was the response.

As she returned to her seat with the coffee pot, from which she poured, then set on a trivet on the table, Samantha couldn't help herself.

"I have to say, Marcie, this intimacy versus distance, this life versus digital make-believe, it doesn't make sense to me."

"I know you think it's callous, our romances, Grandma. We text. We hook up. But I don't think I want anything serious, at least not now."

"But doesn't it leave a hole, not allowing yourself to feel how you really feel? In that void, you might create your own dangerous myth."

"I guess so," Marcie admitted, with a shrug. "In years past, when people went steady..." She paused. "It's just different now – booty calls, hookups, and particularly with the Skype connection, it saves me from having to discuss awkward topics face to face. Don't you see?"

"Without that personal vulnerability, my dear granddaughter, love will never have a chance." Samantha leaned over to hug Marcie, as they heard the toot of the Uber driver's horn. Marcie made a small, sad moue, and then with a toss of her head, exclaimed. "Don't worry about me Grandma. I'll be just fine."

In minutes, her sweet, conflicted Marcie was gone to a reality that Samantha found unfathomable. Or was it she, Samantha, who was the conflicted one?

THIS WAS THEN

INFAMY - 1941

After the usual Sunday dinner of lamb, her doctor father expertly carving the roast, with potatoes and peas, Samantha went to her room on the third floor of the townhouse at West 114th Street, between Broadway and Amsterdam Avenue in New York City, lay down upon her bed and turned on the radio. She felt lazy, satisfied, sleepy.

There was a male voice: The American fleet stationed at Pearl Harbor in Hawaii had received a crippling blow from Japanese aircraft that had bombed it, starting at 7:55 AM Hawaii time – costing 2,000 American lives, 19 ships, helicopters, planes.

It was Sunday, December 7th, 1941– eight months after the war in Europe had started with Adolf Hitler at the helm.

Samantha was in shock. "Oh my God," she cried out, and ran downstairs to find her father, head bent over his radio. As a man of medicine, she could see the emotion streaming from him and the tears in his eyes.

"Daddy, Daddy. What...what does this mean?"

"America is going to war," he said somberly. "It's war."

It was incomprehensible to her. Samantha was 16 years old, a child of privilege, where life had placed her, but she knew, at that moment that a great shadow was across the world.

Samantha's brother, a freshman at Yale, was of age to be drafted. Her young cousins, too, all four males, were ripe for service.

In the early 40s, with World War 11 at its height, New York City became a shadow box at night – outlined by a river on each side of Manhattan Island gleaming in the moonlight. During the "brown out" of the city that took place every evening, Samantha's father patrolled the darkened streets with a flashlight to check that no interior lights from the apartments and buildings spread into those streets, providing the city as target for Nazi bomber planes. Black velour curtains at the windows inside the buildings shrouded any glimmers.

Samantha found this exercise of her father rather ridiculous because any Nazi plane would have had a perfectly circumscribed New York City – between the two silvery legs of the Hudson and East Rivers - in the light of a full moon.

"Shadow boxing, that's what we are doing," she would whisper to herself, as she peered from the third floor window of her bedroom and gazed at West 114th Street below. "Sparring with an imaginary opponent!"

Starting in 1941, the war years, in spite of their severity, were also romantic – at least for Samantha, as a pretty, young American girl. There were soldierly flirtations, and pride in Rosie the Riveter, who represented the more than six million women who now worked in machine shops and weapons plants and for ship builders across the country, their men in the armed services. These women found a sense of value and a new taste of power. They were "out there" and proud of it.

The shadow box of New York City's brownout –the island outlined and embraced by the East and Hudson Rivers - held a sentimental haze for her. She was lost in the dramatic imagery. The young men called her Sam or Sammy with affection. Leggy, sweet, with a radiant smile, she was eyed by many. Still virginal, she unconsciously provoked quite demented responses in those youthful fellows who seemed to swarm around her like buzzing flies.

From her bedroom window, across from the Columba University campus where her father's townhouse stood, Sammy could see the young men in naval uniform – known as The Ninety Day Wonders - as they marched on the street below. Billeted for three months at the Columbia University campus, where their training also took place, they were destined to go to the Pacific theater, after just three months.

At that time, the US was losing the war in the Pacific, island after island, falling to the Japanese. When it was all over, apparently three quarters of those young men who had marched before her, never came back. 90 days is not a long time to train for such lethal an environment as the Pacific Theater, in the early 40s, but it happened.

Before they left to go over seas, many of the young men discovered Sammy. She would attend – with other girlfriends – Saturday night dances held in the basement of Riverside Church at 125th Street and the Hudson River, – and being so pretty and 'such a swell dancer' – you know, the Lindy Hop, and of course slow dancing – she was highly popular.

In spite of the dire times, there was an innocence to it all. The young men – from across the country – Texas, The Ozarks, The West coast – polite, a bit fearful for their immediate futures –were intensely romantic. And the music! How lovely it was. "I'll be seeing you", "Long Ago and Far Away", "Be Careful It's My Heart", these were the songs Sammy danced to and the songs to which certain of the young men fell in love.

And oh, the soft goodbyes.

To no avail, of course.

But, in spite of a war that was worlds away – separated by both oceans – Sammy was having a radiant if wistful time, in love with love, and virginal to the core, or so she had been programmed to be.

At the time, Samantha belonged to no one – not even to herself.

In those days, a lilting song, a gentle touch, the sound of a molten voice, the hiss of silk as a woman crossed her legs, a lowered eye, a female scent, a mane of wavy hair, the separation between two young breasts, all these, played out within the sexual shadow box. Individually, such small sensory things could arouse a young man without the slightest problem – nor intent. It is just the way the male is constructed, his erogenous zones being so overtly outside in the open air. (Not literally)

EARLY YEARS

Samantha, as a young woman, was lusty, emotional, and full of dreams. But then, the 1940s and 50s, were a continuing time of sexual repression in America, of Puritan leanings in the forefront of culture. Look at the movies. Twin beds for married couples - never a double bed, much less a king-size, in which to cuddle. The heroines on film wore tailored suits and presented a prim and proper demeanor, with hat and gloves to match.

Sammy's mother was a Victorian lady, born in 1893. She was a devoted wife and mother, volunteered at a Thrift Shop for which she accumulated and sorted "rummage" to sell for a specific charity (a medical cause – to please Sammy's father). On Tuesday afternoons, she held a regular bridge party for three friends where the ladies enjoyed chocolate thin mints as they snapped the cards. She named the foursome, "The Minties" in honor of the confection.

Sammy's mother believed that any amount of premarital sex undermined the entire operation. To sum up her rules: Don't. Never look at a man. Don't let him touch you. Never call him on the phone. Don't be at his beck and call, and never, ever pay your way. The only 'yes' you ever say is to a proposal of marriage.

She thought that flirting was permissible but that it was an art – batting eyelashes and a coy looking away.

During the war, in the 40s, Samantha' s mother knitted any number of heavy navy blue sweaters to send to the armed forces. (Samantha did too.) She was a thoroughly worthy woman of her time.

Samantha worried. "I want to get married and have a family, but am I limited to just that destiny – to 'live happily ever after' and disappear completely into the woodwork. Uh,uh. Not me."

Samantha was a pert and wholesome girl with hair and personality the color of sunlight. But she was nobody's fool – with a cockiness that surprised and a strong determination. "Who would want to be known as 'the little woman', or 'the missus' or 'my better half'. No thank you," Sammy said aloud to herself in her room.

Yet, at that time, Sam did not know how to break out of the restrictions society and convention placed on her. She sat passively, as if behind a pane of glass.

SOME PLAYFUL DAYS – SOME NOT SO

Samantha was enjoying her teens in spite of the war. Busy with school (all girls) and, later, at college (all girls), her social life – with many strangers in uniform from far-off states – was filled with the sweetness of flirtation in all its forms – a bouquet of roses, a sly wink, a whistle on the street from a construction worker, a lasting kiss in the back of a car.

There were also old boy friends who courted her, home on leave from some foreign front, who would come to the house on 114th Street on a Saturday. The handsome black, grand piano would be played, lots of Coca Cola served and cookies – all so innocent – and yet suggestive, which made the whole exercise exceedingly sexy. So much was going on underneath the simple festivities... dreams of passion, fears for the future, the unknowingness of what was to come.

Samantha was a movie buff. She went often, on a Saturday afternoon to the local movie theater, The Nemo, down on Broadway and 110th Street.

It was the film, "Now Voyager", produced in 1942, that started Samantha smoking cigarettes. She was still in her teens, but the sight of the hero (Paul Henreid) putting two cigarettes in his mouth, lighting both, then passing one to the heroine (Bette Davis) was sexy and grown-up.

That is what young Sammy wanted to be… sexy… grown-up.

Between "Now Voyager" and the pictures of Humphrey Bogart – always with a cigarette, the dark smoke curling about him, the depth of his voice – and the beautiful Lauren Bacall – the pair as lovers entranced her.

And so did their cigarettes!

In 1943, Sammy entered a girl's college in upper New York State. Because of the austerities of those war years, her four-year college experience was accelerated to two and a half years. The girls were trained (in their blue denim jeans and dark slacks, carrying wooden guns) regularly every morning in front of their dormitories, an exercise in anticipation of later service in the armed forces.

As a freshman, Sammy was popular and gregarious. One of her classmates, Audrey, was a rather dour little blond who seemed to have a real crush on Sammy and would follow her around the campus to the point of irritation.

"Come on, Audrey. What now?" Sammy would stop and ask her.

"It's just that I love to know what you're up to," the girl would say, blushing, timorous. "You're… so… I don't know."

Sam would laugh and say, "I don't know either."

One November day, it was cold and Sammy was in the upstairs lounge of one of the dorms, resting on a couch. She was alone and quite exhausted. The curriculum, because of the acceleration, was intense.

Audrey found her there. She sat cross-legged on the floor at Samantha's feet. She looked so sad and forlorn, that Sammy was alarmed.

"What's up, Audrey?" she asked. "Something wrong?"

Audrey did not answer, but Sammy noticed there were tears in her round blue eyes.

"Hey, what's the matter, kid?" Samantha inquired, kindly. She sat up.

Sammy could hardly hear Audrey's answer, it was so low and prolonged. "Sometimes I feel I am being beaten by chains," and Audrey put her head in her hands.

At this moment, three other girls came bouncing into the lounge and the intense moment between Samantha and Audrey was broken... over, but Sammy knew, it was not done.

As the winter progressed, in the spring there was a dance given at the college – for morale purposes. Of course, a group of sailors had to be bussed in for the event because so many young male friends of the girls were deployed in the services to parts unknown.

The sailors were excited until they realized there was no booze, but they obligingly danced with the girls to the amplified record player in the gym. Many of the girls were pretty – in their evening dresses – off-shoulder, or with slim straps – so the young seamen enjoyed themselves – up to a point and the ball ended promptly at midnight.

Samantha, tired, (she had been one of the organizers of the party), returned to her dorm rooms, which she shared with two other girls. They had a small sitting room with a daybed in the center of the suite.

Samantha grew disturbed as she saw that there were half a dozen girls chattering in front of the open door to her sitting room. When she came to the entrance, she saw Audrey on the day bed, at the back of the room, her wrists covered in blood. She was half unconscious and the girls surrounding the scene were almost hysterical.

The crisis was resolved when the proctor arrived and managed to get Audrey medical help, as Samantha recoiled down the hall. "Oh my God," Sammy was crying. "Why? In my room? What was she thinking?"

Janet Moody, one of Sam's roommates said, "Oh, for heaven's sake, Sammy. Don't you know Audrey is a lesbian? She was in love with you."

With that, Samantha fell to the floor in a swirl of black tulle evening dress.

The following weekend, Samantha went down to New York City on the train to her home on 114th Street and the arms of her mother and father, quite distraught. Audrey was a revelation never to be forgotten.

BLIND DATE

A blind date, in those good old days of the 1940s, was usually promoted by friends, to introduce a single friend to an eligible person, with a dream of romance.

But blind is blind. No one knew. The anticipation was there, and if it 'took', it 'could' lead to the possibility of love.

Not all blind dates were fun. One of the worst experiences Samantha had during that time came at the end of a blind double date, set up by Janet Moody. She had not met the older man who was her companion before this night. The four – Janet, her G.I. friend Bob, Samantha, and the older fellow (balding) named Howard, went to The Copacabana, a popular nightspot on the New York scene.

As the noisy, wearisome evening progressed, Janet and Bob decided to move on, leaving Samantha and Howard at their tiny table, but not for long.

On the ride home in a taxi with Howard, Sammy was literally attacked in the back seat. She was crying out, "Stop. Stop" to no avail. He was strong and determined, his hands all over her body, trying to get under her skirt. She literally was in tears.

The next thing she knew, the taxi swerved quickly to the curb. The driver looked back at the pair in the rear of his vehicle. "Mister, get out... you'd better, unless you want me to drive to the police station. It's only a block away."

Furious, Howard clambered out of the cab, adjusting his clothing, slamming the door.

Sammy recovered herself. She thanked the driver. His only response was one word. "Pig!" and he drove her slowly to her home on the upper West side near The Columbia University campus.

He would not let her pay the fare. "No, Missy. You've had enough for one evening."

The next morning, her father came to her bedroom with a huge bouquet of red roses.

"These just came for you, Sammy. You must have made quite an impression."

"I guess so," she replied, taking the flowers. There was a card.

It read: "Apologies," with no name attached.

When her father left her bedroom, she threw the roses into a wastebasket, and repeated out loud, "Pig!"

How does one define provocation? Incitement? Excitement? Stimulus?

"What did I do to provoke him, excite him? I was just being myself," she whispered. "A plain black dress with sleeves and just a v-neck... black pumps... drop earrings. What in heaven made him act that way?

Blind dates are for ...pigs!"

SHADOWS

Life went on - with drama classes (Sammy's college major), continued drilling in front of the dorm with the wooden guns, occasional weekends at 114th Street, and dates with a soldier or army reject. One such in the latter category was a disaster.

His name was Jimmy, and he had been refused by the military services for a bone spur in his foot. His father happened to know the doctor who gave this diagnosis. In fact, the two men were colleagues in a number of lucrative business deals.

So Jimmy escaped the war.

After a dinner at The 21 Club, Jimmy had taken Samantha back to his apartment for a nightcap of scotch and soda (although she did not drink hard liquor) and, ostensibly, to show her a script he was working on.

In the taxi over to the East side of Manhattan, Jimmy chattered on about his work in progress. "It's for the movies. I have it all cast in my head – Barbara Stanwyck, Fred MacMurray..."

"That sounds like ""Double Indemnity", Samantha responded.

"Don't be so fucking negative!" was his response, which made Samantha extremely uneasy.

"Look," she said. "You'd better take me home."

"Too late," was his answer. "We're almost there."

In the darkened apartment with a window behind which reflected the light off the East River, (he had no black curtain to block it), Sammy could see his movements as he approached her, shadowy, stealthy. He held a highball in his hand. "Want one?" he said, extending the glass.

She shook her head. "Put on some lights, Jimmy," she hissed. Her skin was cold. Her face froze and her body felt it was made of wood. She could not move.

This moment was not like the man who had put his hand on her knee at a dinner party, under the table linen with a smile at his hostess, almost complicit.

It wasn't like the battle going home in a taxicab where her date for the evening was so aggressively pawing at her that the driver stopped and told the "gentleman" to get out.

Here was the predator – stronger than she – determined – fearsome. She had never really liked him, nor seen his charm. "Why am I here?" she thought. This was now. Why had she not trusted her instincts? It was all she could do to stand up straight.

But not for long.

It happened on the floor of his shadowed darkened apartment.

And it was brutal.

"Get off me! Get off me!" she remembered crying, but it was indeed 'too late'. The damage was done. She was bleeding as she waited in the cold outside his apartment for the cab he had called to take her home to 114th Street.

Samantha did not tell her mother, nor did she call the police. It would only make things worse.

In fact, she was ashamed that she had somehow let this happen – to go to his apartment, even knowing her essential dislike of him. She felt terribly alone.

Jimmy called the day after he violated her. She hung up before speaking to him, just as she heard him beg her to call him back. She did not. She could not.

Later, the following week, she received a letter from him. "I know you don't believe me, but I really am sorry, can't forgive myself."

Samantha did not respond to his apology. She realized that Jimmy would probably do it to some poor trusting soul, and that as an abuser, he would probably apologize over and over again for the harm he'd done even as he continued to do it.

THE CASTING COUCH

It was not in a producer's plush office in Hollywood. It was not off the set in a Mexican movie studio after a screen test. It was in a seedy back room behind the small office of a famous Broadway director, on West 46th Street, New York City.

The year was 1947. Samantha had graduated from college and was pursuing an acting career, while at the same time, looking for a job, the paycheck of which would make her independent enough to leave home.

This moment, this rare opportunity to perform before such a notable theater personality as the man before her, was a gift and a test she had longed for. Samantha was nervous. She was actually trembling.

Samantha forgot her lines as she auditioned in the tiny office directly in front of his desk. She had prepared carefully – a long monologue from the play and movie "A Bill of Divorcement" by Clemence Dane. This was a huge moment for any aspiring actress.

The words turned into ashes in her mouth. She was so close – the room so confining. She could have touched the edge of the yellow pad, laid out on the shiny wood of this eminent director's desk.

She fumbled for the words, as she lost concentration, partly because of the intensity of his gaze, as if he were appraising her. She wished so hard for the distance of a stage that lifted the actor out of close proximity to the audience and permitted imagination and the personhood of the character to bloom.

He stood up, a small man in his fifties. Her eyes went immediately to the huge bulge in the crotch of his pants. It seemed to be pointing at her. He was touching it and the zipper to his fly. Samantha was revolted.

"Come with me," he said, in a quiet voice, a strangely passive request at that point in a time that seemed to have stopped. He extended one hand toward her. With the other he opened the door behind him to the room with his 'casting couch'. She could see the low sofa at the far end near a window to the street.

Samantha stood still for what seemed forever but was only for a moment, then found herself blurting through the door to the outer office where anonymous actors were nervously arranged on chairs, past the desk of the receptionist who called, "Just a minute, Miss," as she ran past her.

Outside, on busy West 46th Street, she was panting. For some reason she felt shamed – embarrassed, of course – but yes, shamed... as if this overture from him was her fault. It was like 'gas-lighting'. "Is it my fault? Did I bring this on myself? Did I do something wrong? Was I dressed to provoke? what?... a simple black skirt, low heels, a white blouse? Was he into the schoolgirl look?" she whispered to herself.

All she knew was that the famous director put the shame on her, and Samantha was crushed.

"Why do I accept shame and responsibility for that man's lewd acts," she wondered, as she practically ran up the street toward Broadway. "Why do I feel so ashamed?"

JUNE 1950
WHEN SAMMY MET JOSEPH

By the 1950s, Samantha presented a prim, prudish example of Eisenhower-era repression with her hair in a neat chignon, wearing trim, sexless suits and high-necked dresses. But underneath, she transgressed this virtuous normalness. There was a resilient, cocky young woman lying in wait, impassioned, curious, and ready for adventure.

And it arrived.

She was struck by the intensity of the brown eyes behind black-rimmed glasses that gazed at her as she stood in the doorway.

Samantha had been invited to meet a new gentleman, a Mr. Joseph Kahn, by Sue Wilkof, a friend from work, at Sue's apartment on 57th Street on this soft June evening in 1950.

"Another blind date," Sammy had thought as she waited for the elevator in Sue's lobby. "God help me!"

Sammy had found work at an advertising firm on Fifth Avenue. Sue was her campaign coordinator. The job did not pay much, but she was busy there clipping articles pertinent to their clients from the New York newspapers, and assembling project materials.

The job paid the rent for a 2nd floor apartment of a brownstone building with five stories, on 73rd Street off Lexington Avenue – the cost $250 a month. – not bad for the location but a hit on her budget.

Three nights a week she went to secretarial school, improving her typing skills and learning how to take stenography. Samantha was nothing if not ambitious.

In her off time, she was also auditioning for parts in Broadway plays and in television, a relatively new outlet for actors. Dumont was the producer of soap operas (also new to this media, copying the successful shows on radio), and also crime dramas. The programs were shot live, no taping at that time. Sammy's first part on Dumont was in "A Killer Among Us", a half-hour show, where she played a corpse with her pretty legs sticking out of a closet. She was paid $65 (for a non-speaking part).

Now here she was – this June evening – facing a man that she realized right away would be important to her. It was his eyes...brilliant, intelligent, shining like diamonds.

She just managed to say, "Hello'.

After a drink at Sue Wilkof's, (a Cuba Libra – rum and Coca Cola – for Samantha, a first for her), Joseph took her downtown to an Italian restaurant in Greenwich Village where they shared pasta and chicken Parmesan and a bottle of Chianti. They could not stop talking, Joseph regaling her with humorous stories of the PR business, and she responding with tales of her summer life with family on a lake in Maine.

"It was so pure, the lake... the life there – no telephones – no movies..."

"Sounds boring as hell," Joseph responded.

"Oh no. No. We had to create our own fun and games – and believe me, we did. I had four older boy cousins next door and my brother and other kids on the lake. We played water baseball and built a fort out of cardboard boxes and had a Popcorn Ball at the clubhouse – and I learned to swim and dive and love the water..."

"Hey, hey," he said with a twinkle, "I believe you," which Samantha found very charming.

From there, the two went to the Village Vanguard to hear some jazz in the little *boîte* with Mugsy Spanier playing cornet and a delightful assortment of blues and love songs performed with abandon. Both Joseph and Samantha were into jazz - Miles Davis, Duke Ellington, even Artie Shaw, the swing music of the day as well – the Dorseys, Benny Goodman.

There was an immediate bond and it was only the beginning. The two began to see each other weekly, with side trips to the East End of Long Island, and to Connecticut, where Joseph had associates who quite liked Samantha (but frankly did not see them as a couple).

They listened to more jazz at charming little dens about town, and Eddie Duchin playing luscious piano at the Waldorf Astoria, and enjoyed dinners at The 21 Club. One of their favorite places was the elegant downtown club, Café Society, where the beautiful African-American pianist, Hazel Scott, played songs like "A Foggy Day" and "Round Midnight" and even swing renditions of Chopin and Bach.

It was all very heady stuff.

Within weeks, the first kiss happened. It was a starlit New York night. The weather was cool and the air fresh and clean and the kiss long and dramatic.

Samantha was hooked. So was Joseph.

By early fall, he was staying overnight at her apartment on 73rd Street, in the large brass bed, as she was staying at his apartment on 72nd Street in his king-size modern. It was serious.

So much so, that Joseph, who was notoriously frugal in terms of business, went to Tiffany's and bought his lovely girl a pair of crescent shaped diamond clip earrings (her ear lobes were not pierced), which he presented to Samantha over glasses of champagne down at the Village Vanguard.

Mugsy Spanier (made aware of the gift earlier by Joseph) played the haunting Irving Berlin song, "How Much Do I Love You" on his cornet, as Joseph kissed Samantha and she burst into tears (of joy!).

PUBLIC RELATIONS

In the late 40s, PR was a relatively new kind of business, much maligned by the entrenched advertising companies who looked down on and disdained the new-fangled trade as frivolous and redundant.

Joseph had other ideas! His PR firm – Joseph Kahn Marketing Relations – presented different options for clients wanting to expand their business reach, with fresher strategies, more original approaches.

For example, Joseph personally arranged a promotional event on an autumn evening at a convention for liquor salesmen at a local chic hotel on Fifth Avenue. It was to highlight one of his clients, a renowned purveyor of spirits. After a sumptuous dinner and several drinks, on a raised center stage, a gorgeous showgirl, jumped out of a cake. She was dressed in a skimpy Scotch plaid kilt-shaped bikini, holding high a bottle of Joseph's client's most expensive malt scotch.

"Look at those knockers," one executive in the audience remarked with a lascivious smirk.

"I happen to like what's underneath that kilt," was the rejoinder from his associate.

That is the way these gentlemen spoke in those good old days, but action upon their thoughts usually did not transpire. Oh, yes, sexual harassment by powerful men existed as it has since the beginning of time, but it was less overt, quite often only in the mind of the beholder, but not always, of course.

Another titillating promotion of Joseph's PR firm was that of a pretty model living in the wide window at street level, of a small department store, downtown on 14th Street. She lived there for a week, using merchandise from the store; the newest blender in the small kitchen set-up; the modern desk with the latest typewriter in the living area; new linens on the bed where she slept, in a lacy nightgown–(the moment when she retired drew a large nightly crowd). Again, there was a range of raunchy comments by the onlookers, the males among them drooling with desire, the women, surly and jealous of the model's provocative effect on their men.

"Does she really sleep there?" one young adolescent boy asked his father.

"That she does," was the response. "Watch. In a minute she'll pull a curtain around the bed."

"Damn!" the boy exclaimed.

"Well, you can't really see anything much anyway."

"Yeah, but that lace – it was pretty see-through, Dad. You know I saw her nipples."

"I did too," laughed the father. "I did too," and he smiled and licked his lips.

There were other such expositions. The Circle of Beauty was one, where young models with made-up faces, wearing white satin bras and panties, each with a loose, short white satin robe, circled through an elegant hotel dining room at lunchtime.

Vivid, with varied applications of make-up product, they paraded between the tables in clouds of perfume, as soft music played in the background. After all, exciting colorations, new hairstyles, and bright glosses were the point. (Maybe not for the men in attendance. For the gentlemen, the point lay beneath those satin robes!)

There were not only just ladies-who-lunch attending. There were many executive gentlemen enjoying the view. The male reaction was subdued (even with a martini in hand) because it was midday and many were accompanying their wives, but underneath the linen table clothes, it was a different story, a story of arousal.

"Hey waiter. Bring me another, would you?" one gentleman demanded. Then, in a half-whispered remark to his male companion, he groaned, "I'm beginning to sweat." The slim glass – with olive –appeared on cue and was quickly devoured.

Joseph counted on just such responses. He knew men and their proclivities and how to market goods accordingly, that male desires were what made sales, deals, and brought the exchange of money. As Joseph remarked, to women clients, "All you need to say is 'You too can look like this' and to the men? 'Hey. She can be yours!'"

Clever he was. Joseph. No brilliant, as were his eyes, that bespoke a mind alive with thoughts, strategies, even malfeasance. But the latter did not show – to Samantha (at least, not in the beginning), nor to most of his colleagues, associates, partners – until the shiv went in.

Joseph became more lethal as time went on and far removed from those earlier intriguing promotional escapades. He was master of manipulating perception – always to his advantage - and always below the belt.

TOGETHERNESS

As the summer of 1950 changed into fall, the enchantment of new love continued for both Samantha and Joseph, although there came a moment that she found extremely worrisome.

She thought she might be pregnant. (It turned out she was not.) Joseph had reacted to the idea of a baby with little enthusiasm and made the horrifying remark, "We can always take care of that problem."

Samantha did not want to think of what he meant. She had been through a disturbing experience with her roommate, Janet Moody, during college days. Her friend had an abortion, having been made pregnant by a young soldier who was killed in the Battle of The Bulge.

Samantha had accompanied Janet to a local doctor, named Robinson, in Poughkeepsie, who had serviced other young women in the community and at the college, who brought in a surgeon from a local hospital to do the procedure. Samantha did not see the surgeon. Janet had been taken to a separate room.

After about half an hour, Janet emerged shakily, her face tear stained. She paid the local doctor the $1,000 fee, and before she left, she asked him, "Why did the surgeon speak in whispers? That was the worst part... so spooky."

Dr. Robinson chortled. "Listen, Miss. He did not want you to hear his voice because you might remember it in a court of law. You must know he could go to prison for many years for doing this."

Although this incident had taken place six years before, the intensity of the moment stayed with Samantha and the thought that Joseph would perhaps put her through the same kind of trauma was excruciating.

There was no talk between them of marriage. Samantha kept thinking of her mother's admonitions that she had always considered so old-fashioned, but which she now saw in a new and different light. Suddenly, she felt needy, an uncomfortable feeling to say the least, and one that made her decide to speak to Joseph about the future.

They were dining in his apartment on 72nd Street, in early December. Sammy had made a delicious dish of short ribs in red wine, and there was cheesecake ready for dessert with a bottle of champagne in the refrigerator.

Joseph was enjoying the beef in its pungent sauce with gusto. "Hey, Sammy, this is a keeper… absolutely delicious."

"So glad you're pleased." As she watched him devour the last morsels, she made up her mind that with the cheesecake and champagne, she would address the question head on.

She removed the plates and brought Joseph the bottle and corkscrew with two stemmed glasses. As she set them down, she said, "I want to talk to you."

"Whatever, my dear. This should make the talking easy," he said, holding up a glass with its sparkling liquor.

He was wrong.

As Samantha sat again at the table, after a sip of the champagne on her tongue, she said in her softest voice, "I want to know what's ahead for us." She fingered the crescent diamond earring on her left ear.

"What do you mean?" Joseph replied, busily clearing away the cork, and the wire casing from the bottle top.

"I mean exactly that – what do you see for you and me in days to come?"

Joseph stopped cold. His back was to her, as he stood beside the table. In a harsh voice, he said "You talking marriage?"

"Well…" Samantha was taken aback, although that is exactly what she had been wanting to clarify. "We haven't been together all that long…"

He turned toward her. "You can say that again. What's it been, a few months?"

"I know… but are we a real couple yet? Are we… at least somewhat committed? I mean – these beautiful crescents you gave me… they could use a mate for my finger. Christmas is coming…"

"Look, Sam. You sound so needy. Hey, I really can't handle this right now." He sat down at his place at the table.

"Needy, am I? Why not talk about this? It's only to clear things up."

"I didn't know things needed clearing up." His voice softened. "Aren't you happy, Sammy? Aren't things going great? Don't we have fun?"

"Yes, of course. But it scared me when I thought I was pregnant and you… you indicated we'd get rid of it."

"Well, who needs a baby? Jesus, Sammy. Not now. Maybe never. Hell, I don't know. But you ought to be more careful…"

"You know birth control isn't perfect," she responded angrily.

"Well neither is this relationship," he blurted out, "not if you're going to bug me about babies and marriage…"

Samantha rose to her feet, collected her purse from the side table and left the apartment as fast as she could.

She strode home in a cloud of misgivings, tears pouring, and thoroughly disillusioned. Thank God it is only one block to 73rd Street, she thought through her tears. How cold he had been, how terribly cold.

CHRISTMAS – 1950

Why had she mentioned the holiday to Joseph! Why had she mentioned marriage! Samantha scolded herself. Christmas meant nothing to him, as a Jewish man – although she was sure that, for him, there would be some sort of recognition of the day.

But, to have suggested a ring to match the precious diamond crescent earrings had been beyond stupid! "How dumb can you get?" she would cry out to herself, and there was many a night she wept in her pillow.

She missed him. A lot. It was his bright, often brilliant conversation – about the world, politics and business. And the music they shared had been sexy – even sexier than what they had in bed. He was a novice (or so she thought) as was she. But love among the covers had still been warm and satisfying.

It was the coldness of their final conversation that still galled her and when Joseph called, which became frequent as January approached, she would hang up.

During this time, Samantha began seeing an old boyfriend named Christopher who took her to glamour parties in upper east-side apartments. He worked in finance and although a good dancer, their relationship was strictly superficial, for her just a way to spend an evening, for him to try the ultimate pass. It never went beyond kissing, leaving him seething and thwarted.

One evening with Christopher, at a Broadway performance of "Call Me Madam," Irving Berlin's musical, just as she had risen from her seat, from behind, two long slippery fingers pulled her diamond crescent earring from her left ear.

It had been still dark in the theater, and as she turned clutching her empty ear lobe and cheek, she only saw the backs of people putting on coats and moving on out to the cool early winter night.

"Oh," she cried. "My earring! It's gone..."

Christopher started to look at the floor. "You lost it? It fell off? Maybe it fell down under your seat."

"It was taken... ripped off my ear from behind. I felt the fingers." She was close to tears.

"Oh come on, Sammy," Christopher mumbled, helping her put on her velvet evening coat. "Fingers... huh..."

Samantha was devastated. Her diamond earring had been stolen, desecrated, the symbol of all that had gone on between Joseph and herself. She still had the mate in her possession – lonely and single – but it had to be a pair – just as she and Joseph had been.

The loss made her realize she still loved him. She did not realize her Joseph years were yet to continue. Even though she had met him only months ago, Sammy was in love.

The fact he was a Jew was not what drew her to him. But the fact he was a Jew delighted her. Somehow, it seemed to her, that Joseph's faith (although not deeply held) was a bonus. Their falling out had made her miserable. The loss of the diamond earring seemed the *coup de grâce*.

She spent a somber Christmas at 114th Street, her mother concerned about her daughter, now 25 years old, and too pale and thin for her own good, according to the maternal parent. Her father thought Samantha looked just fine, but then he always did.

Then it was on to the New Year, her job, her auditions, her steno classes at night and the business of living. As the year 1951 moved ahead, Joseph's calls continued and letters arrived at 73rd Street saying how he missed her, that he was 'kind of lost' without her, that he was so wrong to be so uncaring at their last meeting.

At first, Sammy did not respond, but on Valentine's Day, she received at her home a magnificent Tiffany vase filled with pure white roses and a card saying the three words "I love you."

She wept some more, then in her heart, she said "Me too" and picked up the phone. She was not sure why, but Joseph had a charm (mental if you will) that conquered - conquered not only her, but others as well. Joseph could seduce the moon. Colleagues, politicians, young women, old ones too, children, even dogs. He had a bon mot: "How do you eat an elephant?"

His answer: "Bite by bite."

If Samantha was an elephant, he had swallowed her whole, bite by bite, and she did not even notice.

JERMAINE

She had been Joseph's secretary for three years – from 1947 when the PR firm had started. She had been his lover as well. Samantha had met her only twice, had spoken with the low-voiced, rather rude woman on the phone a number of times, and had dismissed her as more a person of his past than any current menace.

Samantha was wrong, even though Joseph had dismissed his secretary (and lover) in a painful scene at the office.

For Jermaine, who had always believed she would be Joseph's wife – (had she been promised that fate by the erstwhile Joseph?), was bitterly opposed to anything 'Samantha'. In fact she hated the young woman with all her being. "I AM his wife," she whispered to herself in the empty bed.

"Shiksa bitch," she exclaimed as she tossed alone under the covers. "That damned blond has moved in on my man. Well, that won't last. I'll see to that."

Sammy had indeed moved in – in reality – to Joseph's apartment on 72nd Street, off Lexington Avenue. It was early spring. Samantha had convinced him to marry in May at the office of a Justice of the Peace in Greenwich, Connecticut. After the ceremony, there would be a lavish dinner party, planned at a pricy nearby restaurant – with friends – mostly colleagues of Joseph's in the PR world and a handful of Samantha's girlfriends. (No family on either side).

Jermaine was not invited.

As spring progressed, Sammy transferred some of her belongings to 72nd street. She discovered remnants of Jermaine: white linen hand towels with the initials in red "J. and J."; a set of lacy lingerie in one of the bedroom bureau drawers; in the kitchen: a mug with "Who do you love?" printed across it – again in red – and the name "Jermaine" in her script at the bottom.

Sammy gathered up all these items, plus a hairy hairbrush she found in the bathroom and plunked them into a cardboard box, which she presented to Joseph one lovely April evening as he sat at his desk in the living room.

"What do you want to do with these?" she asked, dropping the offending carton on the floor at his feet.

He bent over to peer inside.

"Oh, that stuff." Joseph paused. "Stick it outside at the back elevator where we put the trash. It will be taken away tomorrow morning."

"Are you sure?" It seemed appropriate to Samantha, but why did she feel a bit sick at the thought.

"I'm sure," he said with a pixie grin, to which she responded with her own smile, "Really sure?" she asked, at which he rose and took her in his arms.

"Absolutely positive," and he kissed her roundly.

Neither knew that it was Jermaine who had stolen the diamond crescent earring, nor that she had bought herself a cheap gold ring that she wore proudly on the fourth finger of her left hand. "They ain't married yet," she exclaimed, as she had put down her $20 at a local jeweler's. "I was there first!"

FISTICUFFS

It was a mild, late April evening in 1951. The rain had ended when Jermaine saw Joseph walking away from Samantha's townhouse door. The secretary had been ensconced in the doorway of a building across 73rd Street, watching, waiting.

In the pocket of her raincoat, she occasionally touched the glossy surface of a single diamond crescent earring, as if to reassure herself. "It's still there," she whispered.

It was at this very moment, she saw Joseph emerge from Samantha's door, descend the stone steps to the street and head toward Park Avenue. He was carrying a cardboard box.

With a speed she did not realize she had, Jermaine flew across the street and from the rear, attacked Joseph with her fists. He turned to her, totally surprised, and on seeing the person who was hitting him, was filled with resentment and anger.

"What the hell's the matter with you? Stop it, Jerry." He had dropped the box to the pavement and was protecting his face from her clawing hands, but her fist got through the flailing and bloodied his nose.

"God, Jerry. Are you crazy?" He grabbed a handkerchief from his pocket and was dabbing at his face. "You are nuts, kiddo. You need help."

At this point the street was empty of people, but, on looking back, Jermaine saw a couple moving toward them from Lexington Avenue. She drew the earring from her pocket and raised it in front of Joseph, even reaching forward sufficiently to actually scratch his face, drawing more blood, and screaming, "You gave her this! You bastard, you son-of -a -bitch. You gave her these earrings, though she only has one left. Ha, ha. I lifted it off her at the theater. She didn't know what..."

"You are one sick woman, Jermaine," and with that remark, Joseph found himself face down on the wet concrete sidewalk, Jermaine having pushed him with her full force – and she was a big woman.

As she fled up the street toward Park Avenue, just as she left him prone, she threw the diamond crescent earring on the street beside him. "Here! Take it to her. It's got your blood on it."

It lay gleaming in the glow of the streetlight that shone down upon it, a single earring in the shape of a crescent moon with its diamonds sending off sparks. It was on a corner of the sidewalk pavement, which was slick and wet from the earlier rain.

Joseph lay beside it. He let out a groan. He wore a business suit, his striped tie, half undone, askew at his throat. He lay there bleak upon the concrete.

He groaned again. His nose bled, and he had scratches on the left side of his face.

"That bitch!" he moaned, and as he struggled to get up, the couple, passing by, rushed forward to help him to his feet.

"Oh my God, oh my God," the elderly woman cried out. "What happened?"

"You okay, fella?" her companion asked.

"Yeah, yeah," the wounded man mumbled.

"But you're bloody!" the Good Samaritan exclaimed.

"Yeah. I was hit...obviously."

"Who," the woman cried. "Who attacked you?

"Lady, you wouldn't want to know." Joseph picked up the box at his feet and walked haltingly away, left leg aching and a handkerchief to the bloody nose.

"Well," he heard the woman say. "Thanks for nothing," as the click of her heels retreated in the opposite direction. No one had noticed the diamond crescent on the pavement.

Of course later, after Joseph had been discovered by the couple and left the scene, Jermaine returned. She had bitterly regretted leaving the earring there on the street or worse still, in Joseph's possession. The earring was there, untouched, with no blood on it, because it had landed in a pool of leftover rainwater.

"Ah, clean as a whistle," she said with relief, as she put the gleaming diamond crescent in her raincoat pocket. "And back where you belong. Maybe I'll have you made into a necklace, my pretty," she said aloud, clutching the crescent tight in her fist. "At least that's something!"

CONFRONTATION

Jermaine had made up her mind to face Samantha before her arrangement with Joseph went any further. The fact that this woman was moving in her possessions to Joseph's apartment – lock stock and barrel – was reason enough for Jermaine to be outraged.

And she was! Livid! Vicious! And as an unscrupulous person, with a fertile mentality, ready to take on her competitor with claws bared.

She called Samantha, one day, the beginning of May, and asked her to lunch.

"It's important," she told the unsuspecting Sammy. "There are things you should know about Joseph."

"Can't you tell me on the phone?"

"They are too intimate."

"Look, Jermaine. I don't know you very well, but I do know that you and Joseph were close…"

"We still are," Jermaine interrupted.

There was a silence. Then, Samantha asked in a very small voice, "what do you mean?"

"I mean what I said." Jermaine let the statement stand in the air, quivering above the conversation. Then, she continued, "Don't you really think we should meet on this?"

"Where?" Samantha asked.

"Why not tomorrow at the Palm Court of the Plaza Hotel. They have a nice ladies lunch. Around 12:30."

"I'll see you there," Samantha answered and rang off. She was devastated by the thoughts put in her head by Jermaine. She barely knew the woman, had seen her perhaps twice and noticed the thick, dark hair cut close to a sharp face, her voluptuous figure, and sensed her aggressive attitude.

She knew Jermaine found her a rival because Joseph had admitted that he and Jermaine had had an affair, ("long over", he said), which had not bothered Sammy particularly. After all, he was a grown man with needs. "Jermaine was just 'there'... you know available," he had claimed. "No big deal."

"Did you love her?" Sammy had asked.

"Christ no," was the answer.

Now this suggestion by the discarded lover, Jermaine, that perhaps things were not finite – well, Samantha was deeply disconcerted.

She prepared for the worst.

Promptly at 12:25, she entered the Plaza Hotel's Palm Court and noticed right away the figure of Jermaine, sitting at a small table for two close to the entrance.

"Right on time, I see," Jermaine announced as Samantha approached and sat down. "Better have a drink," she continued, the dark red lipstick glossy on her lips. "I'm going to have a Bloody Mary. Seems appropriate," she said with a stilted laugh. "Don't you think?"

"I'll have one too." Samantha was steeling herself for what was to come. Noticing the gold band on Jermaine's fourth finger of her left hand, she suddenly said, "I didn't know you were married."

"You didn't?"

"No."

"You could say I was... but that has nothing to do with right now."

Their drinks arrived.

"Here's to young love," Jermaine said, raising her glass. Sammy took a long sip of her tomato-vodka concoction. It was delicious, then said, "About Joseph. I assume this luncheon is all about him."

"If you want it to be."

"Look, Jermaine. You asked me here and you indicated there was something you had to say about Joseph. Well, I'm here. It's now. What is it you want to say?"

"It's very simple, Samantha. God, what a name! ... but I digress. About Joseph. Ah yes. I just want you to realize that he is still – how should I put it – he is still with me... oh you know..."

"I don't believe you, Jermaine. Joseph and I have discussed your relationship with him. I know it went on for some time."

"It is still going on," Jermaine said, her voice raised and nasty, enough that a lady at the next table turned and glared.

"I don't believe you," Samantha said firmly. "I believe him."

Jermaine burst out in a raucous laugh. "Believe him? Believe Joseph? God you are a naïve one."

Samantha put down her Bloody Mary. She was angry. "This is getting us nowhere, Jermaine. This... this lunch was a bad idea," and as she stood up, Jermaine rose, thrust her left hand with its gold ring in Sammy's face and shrieked, "Ask lover boy about this!"

With that, Jermaine threw the rest of her Bloody Mary in Samantha's face.

"Why in hell did you have lunch with Jermaine?" Joseph yelled. He was furious.

"Because she wanted to show me her 'wedding ring' – your wedding ring!"

"What?"

"She's wearing that little gold band you gave her."

Joseph stopped his pacing in the center of his living room in the 72nd Street apartment. He stood immobile, shocked.

"I swear I never gave her a ring! Never! Marry Jermaine? You've got to be kidding."

"Well, SHE wasn't kidding! She's wearing a wedding band."

"Christ," Joseph said turning away from Samantha, "I'll bet the bitch bought it herself to torture me... and you!"

"Well today, she did torture me and she threw a Bloody Mary in my face – ruined my new white blouse..."

Joseph approached Sammy as tears started to drip from her eyes, slow, salty tears. "Oh darling, I promise you I've never been married – much less to Jermaine. Christ, she was just convenient and so fucking eager – and there. I never for one instant loved her."

"She thought you did," Sammy sniveled.

"No way. I knew she always wanted more – but after I met you and pulled away from her, she acted crazier and crazier."

"She's positively scary," Samantha said. In spite of the fact she realized she was blubbering and almost incoherent, she believed him. He was Joseph, her Joseph, and Jermaine was an aberration from the past.

JOSEPH

Samantha and Joseph married on a beautiful afternoon at the end of May in 1951, a quick ceremony in front of a judge in Greenwich, Connecticut. After the ceremony there was an elegant dinner with lobster and *crèpes Suzette* at a superior local inn. There were twelve in all at the table and the champagne flowed, jokes were told, toasts were raised, and with many an air-kiss, the group drove happily home.

As time went by that summer, Samantha found herself agreeing with, catering to, and fawning over her new husband. She subordinated herself, leaving her acting aspirations in the dust, her devotion to Joseph subservient. He had indeed swallowed her whole.

Joseph was charismatic, not handsome but with his deep-set brown eyes (behind black-rimmed glasses), a smile with white teeth, a delightful sense of humor, people gathered around him. He held court.

And he also knew how to listen!

Sammy was mesmerized by Joseph. More important than their sexual life, it was his mind that dominated her. He had absorbed her. She lost herself.

Early in October, she found she was pregnant. Her delight was tempered by how Joseph would react, and predictably, he was negative.

"So soon? Christ. We just got married! A kid? I feel trapped."

This led Samantha into a depressed state that was difficult to shake but sufficiently severe to contribute to miscarrying her baby – or so she blamed her frame of mine.

Joseph was of course relieved and not particularly sympathetic. "We've got time, babe. Plenty of time."

And as that time went by, one year, two years, three years – and still no new pregnancy – Sammy felt alone and at loose ends.

It was only after a visit from her dear college girlfriend, Janet Moody, over a summer weekend at the house in the Hamptons that Joseph had bought the previous year, that Samantha's sense of purpose revived.

"You, Janet. What do you want?"

"You mean – in a relationship?"

"Yes," Sammy responded.

Janet threw her head back. The two young women were in the screened patio off the living room that looked out over Long Island Sound towards Dune Road. They each had morning coffee cups in hand.

"Well, I suppose monogamy comes first. But at the same time I know I would have to fight the urge to cheat..."

"What?" Sammy sat up.

"Sure. I crave the seductive dance. Never again having that... you know, excitement in anticipation..."

Samantha could not help but laugh. "But, really, Janet. You expect monogamy from him but not yourself?"

"I know. I know. It's silly. But, honestly, don't you think we females have a libido as strong as – or stronger than – males? You know, the libido thing in a relationship (how I hate that word 'relationship'), it's often the man's problem, not the woman's."

"I suppose so." Samantha rose and refilled their coffee cups from the pot on a tray on the side table. "In the old days, men were supposed to try to go all the way and women were supposed to hold the line. If she failed, he got to boast and she was awarded the scarlet letter." Both started laughing and sipping their black coffee.

"I have to tell you a funny story," Janet said. "It was when I had just finished college It was summer in Texas and before looking for a real job,

I decided to take the warm months, get a part-time evening job and enjoy the swimming pool during the day. So I go into this bar..."

"A bar?"

"Sure. The name of it was 'The Golden Lasso' – I'll never forget it," and Janet was grinning from ear to ear. "I thought, with a job, I could pick up a little extra cash. I was still living at home. Anyway, the place was almost empty 'cause it was only 4:00 o'clock in the afternoon, and it was not too seedy looking although it sure smelled of beer." She paused.

"Go on, for heaven's sake," Sammy said.

"The manager came out from behind the bar and in a matter of minutes he said, 'You're hired.' He was staring at my breasts. 'You'll be working for tips in the beginning, so if I were you, I'd show off more of your assets,' said with a leer. 'And smile a lot. A man drinks more if he thinks you're listening, so lean in – especially in a low-cut dress.'"

"You're kidding! He was that obvious?"

"For real. He kept saying, 'this is a bar'... oh, he also added, 'if he asks your age, it's nineteen. And hey, after all, how it goes, that's up to you.'"

Samantha took a long drink of her coffee, set the cup down, and responded, "What a crass..."

"Oh, come on, Sammy. They are all alike - beastly and particularly, where you have a job – not just in a bar – for them, sex is ... I don't know. Somehow, it's political - a transaction." She took a gulp of coffee. "Supposed 'consent' in a patriarchal workplace – well it's a farce."

"It's ridiculous."

"No," Janet said. "It's sad. When men are in power, it goes to their testicles!"

Samantha burst out laughing.

"It's not really funny. It's sad," Janet said. "Women have been suckered into a pathetic sense of submission because they don't want to be seen as man-hating prudes."

"I guess because those sexy, domineering males are potential mates, after all," Sammy said with a laugh.

They were silent for a moment, then Janet said, "And you, my friend, how is it with you?"

"What do you mean?"

"With Joseph?" Janet asked softly.

Samantha was taken aback. Somehow the whole conversation about men and their sexuality did not permit her to associate Joseph with any of it.

Sammy stood up. "Things are fine."

Janet was quiet, then, "Don't mean to pry. Just wondered."

At that moment, the man in question appeared.

"OK ladies, let's get ready for the beach. We'll get some lunch at the Swordfish Club," he declared, snapping a beach towel. "I'm ready, as you can see. Go get into your suits."

And they did.

"You're not the same Sammy I remember," Janet remarked over her shoulder as she was packing her suitcase in the guest bedroom, preparing to leave. "Not the Sammy I remember at all."

"What?" Sammy was shocked.

"No!" Janet sat down on the nearest chaise. "It's 'yes, Joseph,' 'No, Joseph,' 'Please, Joseph.' And he puts you down all the time, practically telling you to shut up! Where is the feisty old Sam, my friend and playmate? Where is she?"

After Janet took her leave, Samantha realized she was in a shadow box – on display, objectified. Behind that pane of glass, she was protected but not really alive. She had to face the truth. Janet's words had brought her an epiphany. A new resolution took over.

She thought, 'I have to fight the imaginary opponent to regain myself. It happens to be my own husband, not imaginary at all, but someone I go to bed with, share breakfast with in the morning, festivities at night (always based on his business) and late night suppers'.

Joseph! A paltry man was he, not to be catered to or fawned over or compelling passivity. "Every one of us women is a change maker in her own life," Sammy said out loud.

Gradually, life changed for Samantha. Over time, she retrieved herself, so much so that her husband, Joseph, claimed, "Sam, I'm in a double war! I leave in the morning to the chaos of the business stage, only to come home to a second front! What in hell's the matter with you?"

"Nothing, darling," was her inner response. "It's just that I'm back. I'm a new Samantha, stronger than ever before."

She wondered why. Did Joseph's resentment of her outside activities (a couple of charities she was passionate about; a record company she had invested in) contribute to her newfound sense of strength? Had his not supporting her – and perhaps her not supporting him – or so he had made clear – increased her power, thus infuriating him?

His response to her projects was classic. "You're supposed to be promoting me, not some outside business or dumb charity. You should spend time on the marriage!"

No matter, she decided. What marriage? It had been a long time that communication between them had broken down. The inevitable came about over a five-year period. Divorce papers were drawn.

Joseph was so enraged – divorce had been Samantha's request, not his – that he tried to get his lawyer to have his young wife committed because "Nobody leaves me! Nobody!"

His lawyer, a member of a prominent theatrical law firm, explained that Samantha had no habits, faults, or incidents that could possibly 'get her committed', at which pronouncement, Joseph fired the lawyer.

His second legal choice gave Joseph the same advice and finally, papers were signed and Samantha set off alone for Reno. She stayed at Lake Tahoe for the six weeks needed to complete residency, after which she went to court in Reno and soon enough returned to New York City, a woman far more cautious. Her new independence presented a challenge that at first seemed daunting.

"Okay, World. I'm ready to take you on - I hope. Anyway, ready or not, here I come!"

INTERLUDE

RESTORATION

Ah, how Samantha needed it.

She had given up the idea of acting for good and was working in an advertising firm, living in a small one-bedroom apartment in the East 80s, and trying to cope with a wounded ego and disillusionment. Her divorce in Reno, after a six-week residency, had been a searing experience.

But it was over and she was back working overtime with Sue Wilkof, and her former employer, Nancy Smythe, who valued her performance and admired her courage. Samantha was earning good money. She had gotten a sizable Christmas bonus, but she still cried at night because of what she called 'the Joseph syndrome'.

How he had torn her down?

How she had allowed it to happen?

Where was her core persona?

Was there one?

She must find out.

She had allowed a man to absorb her. With Joseph, it had been bite by bite. With another, would it be the same, that she would dissolve and disappear?

Her despair was compounded when her college friend, Janet Moody, called her from Texas and told her that Audrey – the girl with the bloody wrists – had committed suicide.

Samantha was exhausted. It was the work, travel, the move, and new responsibilities. It was Joseph. And now, it was the death of a poor, benighted young woman whose sexuality had made her feel 'beaten with chains', a pain so strong it made her take her own life.

For Samantha, it was almost too much to bear.

She decided she had to remove herself from this apartment, this workload, this city. She would go to France – to the storied world she had always dreamed of, where the tales of the landings in Normandy and the bravery of men and the broad Champs-Élysées beckoned. She longed to find herself there, to grow up and out, to feel in her own skin, and though her expectations were high, somehow Samantha felt she would not be disappointed.

So, she counted her dollars, changed some to francs, bought a ticket on the SS *Liberté,* a small French liner aiming for *Le Havre,* gave notice at the advertising firm and left the city of her birth with a heart full of hope.

The *Liberté* replaced the great French liner, *Normandie,* as flagship for the French Line. The *Normandie* lay in ruins at the bottom of the sea, due to German U Boats during World War 11.

Samantha found the trans-Atlantic crossing thrilling, with its music in the evening, and caviar at the dinner table and the fresh breeze off the ocean.

It was the fall of 1960. She had just turned 35.

PARIS

Samantha arrived in the City of Light in the warm November of 1960. It was the perfect incubator for her – a place in which she could lick her wounds, adjust to a *divorcée's* life, assess her choices of the past and grow up.

Her imagination was whetted by the whole Paris scene. She managed to find a small apartment on the Left Bank, near the *Musée Rodin*. The address was *Onze, rue Monsieur,* a fitting name, she thought.

One entered through a courtyard, and her rooms were up the stairs on the third floor – a lovely sitting room, a large bedroom with walk-in closet, tiny kitchen and bath. "Perfect," she said to herself, and it was.

Of course, there were moments of loneliness and a kind of despair, at which times she wrote rather sad poetry. Her acting ambitions were long gone, but her sense of drama and myriad talented gifts still pertained.

She took a six-week course at the *Cordon Bleu* and learned to cook some elegant dishes – from omelets to *crème brulée* with its crusted sugar top. She developed a taste for the beautiful French wines – *Cabernet Sauvignon, Pinot Noir* – a taste so strong that in later life, even with the best Italian pasta dinner, she always served French wine.

She had a handsome, married French lover who filled her evenings (met him when she tripped coming out of the *Louvre* and nearly fell into his arms).

"Quelle chance!" he had said, so delighted was he with this pretty

young woman in his embrace. *Pierre* was a well-respected doctor, a Frenchman whose mother happened to be British.

"*Quelle chance* indeed!" Samantha remembered saying, equally delighted with the encounter.

During the lovely evening trysts the two began to enjoy, Samantha learned the ways of love, and began to realize how deeply Joseph had in fact abused her – oh, not with his fists – but with his demeaning of her human-hood, her woman-hood - how he would demand that she come home from lunch for a "nap" whenever he wished, – whether she wanted to or not – so cold, so peremptory, so unsexy! And how cruel he had been over the miscarriage, how dismissive of having a real family. Somehow, Joseph never empathized with her sense of loss. 'He never knew who I was,' Samantha said to herself.

Joseph was a man jealous of anything or anyone that drew attention away from him, an ego so pathologically drawn, that he only knew the offensive, had no idea of compromise or forgiveness, certainly not in terms of his young wife, Samantha.

And Jermaine! Samantha wondered if she and Joseph had gotten back together again, but in fact, it meant nothing. Sammy cared not at all. "They deserve each other!" Her Bloody Mary confrontation with Jermaine had given Sammy all the information she needed about that malicious and untruthful woman.

Samantha's 'prim' quality transformed. She bought a formfitting Balmain suit, right off the model. It was made of black silk with a bronze colored velvet collar. She purchased an evening dress in dark blue satin with a white taffeta bandeau across the breasts, leaving her shoulders bare.

These exquisite clothes expressed a new femininity and made her walk with pride. Her 'hang-headed' stance (Joseph's influence) was gone for good and all.

With *Pierre,* her sexuality bloomed, flourished, but his handsomeness and charm frightened her from anything permanent. Besides, he was married and strangely enough, she was glad about that, although at first she felt she had fallen into the classic trap. The extra-marital affair in

France – *l'autre femme* – the other woman – in song, in film, in reality, was accepted and understood, dramatized and, yes, expected.

Samantha suddenly felt French and it was delicious. There was not a shred of guilt.

One evening, her *Docteur* had to stop by a hotel room to look in on a young English woman who had taken sick (a sore throat and fever). She was the daughter of a British friend of *Pierre's*.

"It will only be a minute," he explained to Samantha, as he picked her up for their dinner date. "I've never even met her. Then, you and I are off to *Le Petit Clos*. I know how you love their *canard confit, ma petite*."

When they entered the hotel bedroom, the face of the young woman among the pillows turned bright pink, at the sight of the stunning Frenchman leaning over her and taking her pulse. She could hardly speak – except in a small panting voice.

Samantha knew there and then that any thoughts of longevity were not to be considered. With *Pierre*, any time away from him would be fraught with anxiety, not from him making a move, but from predatory women.

She accepted this and made up her mind to love as best she could, in the moment.

"I'll wait for The One to come along," she exclaimed to herself.

"Or Not." And somehow, for the first time, she realized that would be okay. "I have ME."

THE FRENCH DENTIST

Samantha developed an excruciating dental problem – an impacted wisdom tooth. She asked her *Docteur Pierre* for the name of a dentist and rushed off to an emergency appointment *chez Le Dentiste Jean Trudier,* a renowned gentleman dentist to the Paris elite.

On arriving, Samantha realized there was no nurse, but *Le Dentiste Trudier* was deferential and *sympathique* as he made her comfortable in his lay-out chair, tied a paper bib under her chin and proceeded to inspect the offending tooth in her mouth. He would turn her chin gently but then began forcibly trying to extract the molar, a wisdom tooth at the back of her mouth, with what looked to be a pair of pliers.

"Ow!" Samantha exclaimed. "That hurts."

"Ah, Madamoiselle, it is not so easy to pull out...*un peu de temps encore...* and he continued to dig at the gum under the tooth.

Samantha noticed that, in order to gain traction, the dentist's right leg had risen to cover the lower part of her body, as she lay stretched out in the dentist chair. This was totally unexpected and a sudden alarm went off in her head.

"S'il vous plait, monsieur"...and she pushed vigorously at his leg with both hands. She realized with dismay he was trying to mount her because he resisted her efforts and the second leg was on its way to cover her body.

It was particularly distressing because the tooth was only halfway out and the *dentiste* had the advantage for sure.

"Non, monsieur. Non. Non. Non!" Samantha's face was red with anger, and

she shoved him off her with strong arms and a determination he accepted. He said nothing, but with a final pull, extracted the tooth. He attended to the cleansing of the site, silent all the while, packed it, and finally said, "*Fini*".

Samantha clambered down from the dental chair, smoothed her skirt and as she turned to leave, *Le Dentiste Trudier* said, "*Madamoiselle*, pull down your pants."

"What?" Samantha was shocked.

"You heard me. Pull down your pants." He was preparing a syringe. "I need to give you a shot in case of infection."

Samantha, so undone, did as she was told, pulling down the pink girdle under her skirt, exposing her buttocks. He gave her the shot, after rubbing a spot in the girlish flesh with antiseptic. She quickly pulled up the girdle.

"You should not wear such an item," he said in accented English, "breaks down the muscles. You should wear plain, light silk panties."

Ugh, was all she could think as she hurriedly paid the bill and took her leave, walking thankfully in the Paris April mist.

Her mouth hurt, but the tooth was out, she had not been raped, and was thankful to reach her apartment at *Onze, rue Monsieur.*

'What is so sexually provocative about a bloody open mouth,' she thought, 'or was it his sense of power as he hurt me? Either way, the French *dentiste* was a disgusting creature!'

On flopping down on the couch, she reached for the phone and called *Pierre* who had recommended the good *Dentiste Jean Trudier.*

After relating the whole experience to her trusted lover, Samantha was astonished to hear him comment, "Oh, I thought he'd gotten over all that!"

It was a shock, this comment. For the first time, Samantha thought maybe it was time to go home. *Pierre* had been her recovery. She was grateful and suffused with the pleasure of his company. But enough was enough. "'I thought he'd gotten over all that?'" she repeated out loud. "*Ah, mon Pierre. Ça suffit.* You too are just a typical man. I thought you were more. Ah well. *Tant pis.*"

Strangely enough, his attitude made Samantha's desire for him absolutely disappear. Yet, *Pierre* had indeed been there to restore her ego and sense of self. For that, she would always be grateful.

She booked a flight home for the following week.

PAN-AMERICAN AIRWAYS HOME

Samantha had a window seat on her flight back to New York City. On looking out at the luminous clouds, her thoughts were of lost love, how heartbreak is a dangerous emotion and commitment a risk.

She was thinking of the men she had known: father, first and foremost, her remote but admirable father; brother, war veteran and always supportive; four boy cousins, a little older, there to play with, have fun, tease and enjoy.

Then there were the boyfriends, casual and not so; the aggressive ones, in the back of taxis, on the dance floor, in darkened apartments; then Joseph. Now he was a story all to himself.

Next *Pierre* who taught her the pleasures of love, and helped her understand the whole ambiance of Paris. It was a city that enthralled her with its sensitivity to the sexual world and all the nuances of romance, also, the cynicism (*la dentiste*) and hard cash realism that can accompany *la vie d'amour.*

On sinking back in her seat, covered by a blanket, she decided, "enough of that" and instead revisited in her mind the cities she had been able to experience in her months in Europe – glorious Rome with its ruins still alive – and the pasta! (There, Samantha had enjoyed the Italian wines –*Valpolicella,* even *Chianti*) - the smell of garlic in the air, the warmth of the people; the golden aura of Florence; and Barcelona with always the sound of flamenco – even in the streets; and London, where she had spent Christmas and had eaten a Christmas goose.

Of course there was the epic city of them all - Paris - where she had retrieved and put together the rather shattered person that she once had been – thanks to *Pierre* and her charming little apartment and the *Musée Rodin* gardens full of roses and brilliant statues – and the embracing *bistros* with their easy familiarity and wonderful *soupe à lioignon* and ah yes, the wine.

Samantha felt blessed, and fell asleep in a happy state.

When she woke, the flight attendants were serving lunch – a not bad salad, a browned piece of chicken – and a glass of red wine – and Samantha addressed her thoughts to the immediate days ahead.

She planned to go back to the same townhouse in the 80s where she had had an apartment (on a monthly lease). She hoped the same one might be available, although it was unlikely. Perhaps there would be another on a different floor. The landlord and she had gotten along well. That should help. Until she found a place, she had just enough money to stay in a hotel, if necessary.

But the 80th Street location would be perfect. On the top two floors (there were five stories to the building), her friend, Richard Green and his wife, Anne, lived with two young sons. Richard had been a resident there for a long time, since college days. His friendship might help too.

Samantha and Richard had known each other at college where he was assistant stage manager and set designer in the drama department where Samantha was taking her major. Often, on a Saturday, the two would sneak down to New York and to Broadway and see a play – a special outing that drew the two close. Samantha realized early on that Richard was gay but pretending he wasn't. Needless to say, they did not discuss it, but she knew, from just the smallest gestures and phrases he used unconsciously that he was homosexual.

So it was a surprise that he married. It was at the same time in 1951 that she had married Joseph. Richard had found a beautiful model who worked for Norman Norell, one of the great American designers.

Anne was lovely and Samantha discovered that she had a brother who lived with another man in a house they bought in Boston – quite a scandal at the time.

So Anne was inured to shock and awe over gayness. And then to have two sons! The little family were great friends of Sammy's and the little boys were surrogate children for her to dote on, having none of her own.

One of Samantha's deepest concerns was having a child. She was now in her mid-thirties. She had always wanted to be a mother and time was running out.

Being able to play with little Richie and the smaller Andrew Green was a special gift that Richard provided for his friend. After the sweet moments with the two little boys, whether at the zoo in Central Park, or over ice cream sundaes at Schrafft's, Samantha would feel an enormous hole in her life and in her being, a physical emptiness. Yet she adored being with Richard's children.

Samantha loved Richard and Anne for allowing her the precious time she spent with the little boys. Thinking back, she remembered the initial shock she felt when she learned that when Richie was born in 1955, while Anne was still in hospital, a young man had moved into their 80th street 5th floor apartment for a 'visit' with Richard.

It was never discussed.

The plane was soon to land. Samantha continued her plans for the days ahead, with a projected visit back to the advertising firm and to her previous boss there, Nancy Smythe, to see if she could return to her job. Of course, her parents were first on her list. She had missed them and had bought a special leather wallet for her father and a gorgeous multicolored scarf from *Hermès,* the famous store on the *Faubourg St. Honoré,* for her mother. She was eager to embrace them both.

New York! New York! She could see the Statue of Liberty from the plane window. As she gathered her carry-on and purse together, she remembered in April, 1945, standing on a hill overlooking the Hudson River and the railroad tracks below, holding a candle – with Richard Green at her side. They awaited the train, carrying the body of Franklin Delano Roosevelt to his resting place at Hyde Park. The railroad car in which his body lay, was covered by a huge American flag, as the train crept slowly towards its destination, and Richard Green held her hand.

New York. New York. Samantha moved down the aisle of the plane. Now, in her mind was the picture of the glorious kiss of the sailor and unknown young girl in Times Square when World War 11 was over. She was home, and somehow she knew love awaited her, too.

THE WHISTLE

Early spring in New York is always filled with promise, particularly that April day in 1961. Samantha, in her stunning black Balmain suit with its bronze velvet collar, walked down Madison Avenue toward the advertising firm, for her appointment with Nancy Smythe.

She had already been to her parent's apartment for an early breakfast of eggs and bacon. Her grand presents from *Hermès* in Paris were a delightful surprise. "You look wonderful, darling," was the view of both mom and dad. Neither had been thrilled with her marriage to Joseph and both her parents were glad Samantha was now a free agent.

"Paris did it, Mom. I feel rejuvenated."

"Well, you look it!" her mother exclaimed.

Samantha bid them a fair farewell. "See you for dinner Sunday. Leg of lamb, Dad?"

"You bet," was his answer.

Now, with head held high, enjoying the wispy rays of sunshine, Samantha was singing to herself. She passed a group of four construction workers, as they attacked the base of a building with various instruments, shoring up the concrete. All four paused in their work to give her the once-over.

"Hey, pretty lady," they said, almost in a chorus, which was followed by a loud series of whistles.

Samantha smiled, gave a little wave of the hand and proceeded on her way, a dance in her step and a grin of pleasure on her face. "I guess I look okay today," she said to herself with a glow of satisfaction.

And she did look okay that day, enough to retrieve her job, with an increase in salary!

"You look fabulous," was Nancy Smythe's remark as Samantha entered her office. "Paris really did you good."

"You can say that again," Sammy replied. "It brought me back to life."

With her job secured, to start at the beginning of the next week, Samantha made her way to the 80th Street townhouse where she hoped to regain her old apartment on the first floor. It was taken, but she was able to sign a monthly lease for one on the third floor, with the exact same room layout, and for the rent: $300 per month.

She did not call Richard or Anne. She decided to surprise her old friends after she had moved in.

She returned to her room at the somewhat seedy hotel downtown, where she would stay for another two nights. As she removed the black Balmain suit and hung it up carefully, put on jeans and a tee shirt with a large imprint of PARIS printed on it in bright red, she said out loud, "What a day - all brightened up by those whistles!"

INTERLUDE INTERRUPTUS

Joseph!

Not only did Samantha run into him on Fifth Avenue, one rainy Wednesday afternoon at the end of April, but she had had a disturbing conversation with Richard Green about the man, only days before over the week-end.

She had asked Richard to lunch on Saturday, (Anne was working) and had prepared, in her newly acquired rooms on the third floor, an elegant *Salade Niçoise* and *Mousse au Chocolat* for her good friend.

He was delighted with her efforts, and even happier to see her and hear of her adventures. Then, he was quite frank with Samantha. "You know I never liked Joseph… at least, not for you. Oh, he had his charm, but really, my dear, he is one tough *hombre…*"

Samantha laughed. "You can say that again."

Richard then told her of the rumors about Joseph – of frequent infidelities that were characterized as meaningless encounters, adding that "Joseph is the kind of man who, while staying at a hotel, will order up a whore for breakfast."

"Ugh," was her response. "I'm not surprised."

Samantha, toward the end of the marriage, had guessed Joseph's sex on demand had not applied only to her. And he did travel… a lot. This new information did not bother her particularly. At the time it was all happening, her submissiveness had protected her. With commitment and any passion gone, she had been numb to Joseph-facts.

When she loved him, she had loved him in a child-like, patriarchal way, but that seemed long ago. Paris – and *Pierre* had restored confidence and helped develop in her a new maturity.

Joseph!

But now, there he was – standing in the covered entrance of a large building, here on Fifth Avenue, and she was directly opposite, stark-still in the pedestrian traffic and the rain drops under a large black umbrella.

It was a shock to see him.

Within seconds, as their eyes met, right behind him, Samantha glimpsed the figure of Jermaine emerge from the building's entrance. She came up to stand beside Joseph. The three were glaring at each other.

Even through the wet sheet of rain, Samantha could see a crescent-shaped diamond hanging on a platinum chain around Jermaine's throat. It fell deep into her cleavage, which was – even on a rainy day – always prominent and on display.

The stolen diamond earring! Samantha still had its mate.

Jermaine put one hand on her hip, while the other fingered the brilliant crescent. There was a slight smirk to the red lips as she eyed her former rival. She half leaned against Joseph, as if to say, "He's mine!"

Samantha noticed that there was a gold ring on the fourth finger of Jermaine's left hand.

Was it for real? Were they married? "She's just... there, Jermaine," he had said. "No big deal." What a liar.

But the gleam of the diamond crescent beckoned to Samantha. When he had given her the pair of earrings, it had represented their love. Now, all the crescent around Jermaine's neck reminded her of were the insults and disgust that clouded the distance between the two women. It filled her with a rage she was unused to and which she refused to accept.

Samantha was newly out of the box that had confined her – Joseph's box of glass. Or at least, her strength was growing sufficiently to soon enough crash through and be finally free.

No one spoke during that moment on Fifth Avenue. Time seemed frozen. Slowly, Samantha felt her legs move beneath her and she began to walk again, at a leisurely pace, a casual posture, away from the pair beneath the entrance of the building. She did not look back.

As she walked, her stride lengthening with confidence, she pondered her expanding world. Since her return from Paris, not only her job, preoccupied her, but, her life was filled with promise.

She had become a member of the board of an African Medical Research Foundation, the flying doctors who did magnificent work on that continent, training the native people, as they spread their expertise and medical skills. It was an eye-opener. She met extraordinary doctors, many African-American. She became great friends with Edna Mae Robinson, Sugar Ray's ex-wife, a beautiful woman with a delightful sense of humor who was on the board. She met Gordon Parks, the Life photographer who had pictures at MoMA. Through him, she even met her idol, Miles Davis.

Samantha had also become involved with a no-kill Animal Shelter on Long Island. Her love of dogs was fulfilled by this latter commitment. In fact, she was planning their latest fund-raiser gala, to be held at the Pierre Hotel.

Samantha would have to make a speech at the Pierre event. Her old acting chops would come in handy. She would wear her blue satin evening dress with the white *bandeau* across the breasts and with these happy thoughts, her confidence at its height she entered her office building, Joseph, Jermaine, the diamond earrings long forgotten.

At least for now.

A PIERRE HOTEL GALA

It was a glorious event, to Samantha. As chairman of the Animal Shelter fund-raiser, she had ordered the menu: lobster cocktail, followed by a choice of sole in butter sauce or roast beef, and a succulent cheesecake served with fresh berries and whipped cream.

The dance floor was full; the music pulsing and delightful. The speeches were over. There were dogs in attendance – police dogs, seeing-eye dogs, therapy dogs, even personal pets. And every animal was well behaved.

Not so with some of the people as it turned out.

Samantha knew she looked her best in the beautiful dark blue satin dress, her creamy shoulders rising above the white *bandeau*. She circulated, conversed with many a donor, and was having a fine time.

Suddenly, she saw, coming toward her, in fact dancing their way across the floor to the lovely song, "Just in Time", Joseph with Jermaine in his arms, crescent diamond at her throat. They stopped abruptly, directly in front of her.

"Well, Joseph," Samantha had the temerity to say. "I hope you're having a grand time and will give a big donation." This was said with a dazzling smile.

He did not respond but was staring at her, as if for the first time. Samantha knew he saw her brilliant new self in a different light. Jermaine looked sullen. "We'll give something to the doggies," she muttered, and she fingered the crescent diamond earring that hung on its chain around her throat as she had before. Her gown was a garish floral print, and her body was revealed in a most flagrant way.

The difference between the two women was notable. Jermaine looked cheap. Samantha had class, and Joseph could see the difference. Boy, could he. His face turned red, and with the song, "Just in Time" still playing, he grabbed the crescent diamond earring, and literally pulled it off the chain around Jermaine's neck.

She let out a scream, which stopped the party and shook it into a silence so all could hear Joseph's diatribe. "You bitch," he said to Jermaine. "You stole this from Sammy... actually stole it... and now you flaunt it. You ruined her and me on purpose! Sammy left me." He was sputtering, Jermaine was in tears, and Samantha stood there, with her mouth agape at the scene.

Joseph stepped forward, diamond crescent in hand. "Here," he said to Samantha. "This belongs to you. It always has. It always will." His voice was soft. He took one of her hands and placed the little gem into her palm, looking deep in her eyes.

Samantha clasped it. "Joseph, you're ruining the party. Please..." and she turned on her heel and left him standing alone, because Jermaine had run off to the cloakroom, sobbing all the way.

The crescent seemed to burn in her palm, as Samantha walked back to her table, signaling to the band to please continue the music (which they did, picking up on a jazzy song that made people want to move). She felt empowered, and knew exactly what she was going to do with the now pair of earrings. She would buy a little black velvet box and encase them in it forever, closing them in, never to wear them, never to be reminded of the woman she had been and never wanted to be again.

"I'll never go back," and with a radiant smile, she collected her evening coat from the office, and stepped out into the New York night.

"I'm free of him at last."

THIS IS NOW, AGAIN

A DOUBLE-EDGED SWORD

There is always the abuse of men. Been there forever.

But what of women? They can dress provocatively, wear the sexiest perfume, dye their locks (wherever they grow), and make up their faces as seductively as possible.

All true, Samantha thought as she sat, caressing her little rescue dog, Abbi. "Sexual mistreatment is nothing new," Samantha said aloud to Abbi. "It's now called harassment – lately traced through Anita Hill to the Clinton impeachment, to Harvey Weinstein, to Jeffrey Epstein. And Trump! Good lord, what a list!"

Samantha rose, to fill her coffee cup, then returned to the sofa next to the dog, where she continued to talk to Abbi. (They often had a conversation.)

"Okay," Sammy went on. "But bust implants, butt implants, botoxed lips to puff them up – doesn't this suggest open sexuality? Why do it, unless one wants sexual attention? Aren't these women 'asking for it'? Or is it just to tease? To seek being desired without having to act? It's kind of hypocritical, don't you think, Abbi?" Samantha shook her head, thinking of the quandary this behavior produced. What is a man to think? She wants it? She wants me? Why not try?

"Can't blame him," Samantha said aloud. "It's a mixed message that some women send, for sure. I can just hear her: Do this for me. Don't do this to me. Go where I wish. Wish for what I do. Comply and I will give you the moon. If you don't comply, I will ruin you, your job, your wife, your life."

Samantha picked up her copy of the latest newspaper. On one of the inner pages, she read a story about a conflict between a construction worker and a young woman with an umbrella (although it wasn't raining).

Apparently, the construction guy had whistled as she walked by, to Samantha a compliment, but apparently to the lady in question, "harassment!" for she had gone after the poor fellow with her umbrella (closed), attacking him and shrieking that he was harassing her with his whistles.

Evidently, all he could bleat out was, "Hell, lady, I thought it was a compliment."

"A compliment!" she complained so loudly, that her voice drew a number of other women, who continued to berate the construction guy with all sorts of expletives.

Finally, two policemen managed to disburse the crowd.

"God almighty. This is too much!" Samantha exclaimed out loud to her dog, Abbi, who listened to her mistress attentively. And Sammy sat back on her sofa and remembered the happy April day when a workman's whistle of approbation had led her back to a New York life. Oh, there were other whistles of appreciation in her past – when she was young and vibrant– and why not. The whistle implied desire – but never action! And it always pleased her, made her feel pretty and walk tall.

"That was then," she sighed. "This is now." Abbi seemed to sigh too, as she laid her head on Samantha's knee.

"Sometimes it just goes too far."

MARCIE???

Is that Marcie? Samantha mused as she looked at her granddaughter who had just arrived at the house in Atlanta from the airport via an Uber car. She was dressed in a boxy, rust colored over blouse, with fishnet stockings and boots with high, black platforms. But it was her hair – her beautiful, thick dark hair! It was cut off completely, except for a short trim and black bangs on the forehead.

"Is that you?" Samantha cried, as she hugged Marcie to her.

"It's me, Grandma. It's me. I know I look different…"

"Ah, yes, darling. Indeed you do," Samantha said affectionately. "So different since you were here – what, two months ago?"

"It sure is a lot less hot," Marcie remarked.

"Well, it is September and even in Georgia things cool down a bit."

"A lot has happened," Marcie said, dragging her small suitcase, through the garage, into the laundry room, through the kitchen, and into the guest room. She was chattering all the way. "My life has changed so drastically. I'm living in a different place – have new roommates…oh, Grandma, it's awesome. I've got so many plans… but first, I have to tell you something."

Marcie twirled around, found her purse, pulled out her wallet and her driver's license. "Let's go into the living room."

"Would you like something to drink?" Samantha asked.

"Not yet. In a minute. First, Grandmother, sit down. I have something world-shaking to announce," she said with a huge smile. "I am no longer Marcie. My name is Jake."

"What?"

"Yep. I am Jake Hayes. Legally. See, it's even on my new driver's license. Jake Hayes," she said pulling out the little card from her wallet and sticking it under her grandmother's nose.

Samantha was in a daze. "You're kidding," she managed to squeak out. "I know Maryanna was a mouthful – your mom insisted on that name – but we all called you Marcie...it was easier and so cute and so... kind of feminine..."

"Grandma," Marcie said, standing in front of Samantha, feet in their platform boots spread apart. "My name is Jake. You have to get used to it."

"Well, please Mar... Jake... Give me a minute." Samantha passed back the little card bearing the Jake Hayes name to her granddaughter (or grandson)?

There was a silence. Jake stood arms akimbo. Finally, Samantha rose and said, "Let's get that drink!" and she went to the small bar off the kitchen and made herself a vodka, on ice with Perrier. "Want one?"

"No thanks – but I'll get a Coca Cola," and Jake reached down in the drawer of the refrigerator for a cold can of the soda.

The two went into the living room and sat on the couch, facing one another. Abbi sat between them, looking from one to the other.

Samantha took a long sip of her drink. "Now, tell me. How did this come about... this Jake business?"

"Look, Grandma. I know you're shocked, but times have changed. I'm learning to express myself – my real self – without the confinement of gender. I identify myself as nonbinary. I even use neutral pronouns – they, them – not him/her. I love the architectural look in clothes. It's so neutral."

"I guess it is," Samantha said, taking another long sip.

"And I'm getting testosterone therapy."

Samantha sat up. "Ah, Mar...Jake. You're so young for such a decision... too young."

"No, Grandma, too old! I'm 25, for God's sake. An adult. It should have happened when I was little."

"But you realize what testosterone does to the - dare I say it – female body?"

"Of course. That's why I'm doing it. That's the whole point. My breasts will shrink, my nether parts enlarge, my voice will deepen – and yay... no periods..."

Samantha couldn't speak. After several minutes, she asked, "But I thought you wanted children?"

"Oh, I want a kid. Absolutely. My friend Robin wants one too and they have a boy friend. His name is Pablo. He's Spanish."

"I would assume so," Samantha said, staring into her drink. "'They? I guess you mean Robin?"

"Uh huh. Pablo lives with us. So when there's a child, Robin will carry it. It will have three loving parents... with three sets of wages. None of us will be drowning in care-taking for the kid, and the three of us, fussing over it, that's really beneficial, don't you think?"

"Poor little 'it'!" Samantha shook her head. "God, Jake. It's hard to get my mind around all this. Doesn't it occur to you that three people in the same bed? I mean, what has that got to do with love?"

"But sex doesn't have anything to do with love."

Samantha burst out laughing. "You're kidding," she gasped. "That's a new one. Sex has everything to do with bodily commitment and involves emotion – or should - and that should be part of what we used to call love. Ah, the good old days," and she took another gulp of the rapidly disappearing vodka-soda.

"Not anymore," was Jake's reply. "Sex is a physical, and I must say, an incredibly enjoyable release. It helps you soar."

"Okay. It helps you soar to where... you and your partner... partners?"

"Who cares where? They soar too. We soar together to our separate 'wheres'. Oh, Grandma. It's just... different."

"You can say that again," and Samantha rose and went to the bar off the kitchen for a refill, another way to soar, she thought, and boy, she needed some way to lift her spirits and welcome Jake... Jake Hayes, a new, nonbinary member of the family!

WORDS OF WISDOM? IN THE GOOD OLD DAYS

"If a married man strays – usually with a younger woman – well, she makes him feel younger too. She prolongs his life, staves off his death. He feels there are songs still to sing and that he's younger than spring – to feel the early pulse of life, at least for a moment."

"It's not fair." Samantha, at the age of 15 was shocked by her mother's candor.

"Darling, life isn't always fair." Then, she said thoughtfully, "For his wife to feel younger...? She can go out and buy a new hat – dye her hair – go on a diet."

"And that makes her feel young?"

"Believe me. It helps."

"You sound as if it happened to you, Mommy."

"Perhaps it did," her mother had said with a smile. "Once, your daddy was in love. Oh, I don't think much happened for real, but there was a definite time when he was moody and distracted and remote. I knew. I sensed it. But it passed and was never mentioned."

"What did you do?"

"I already told you."

"You did?"

"Sure. I went out and bought a new hat!"

Samantha, now in old age, remembered this moment with her mother with such affection. Even at that time, her mother was matronly, but also bright, well read, curious, and essentially wise.

She had been the youngest of three daughters, born in 1893, and in those Victorian days when she was raised, the youngest girl was always the last to marry; oldest, first; middle girl, second; and finally the baby, who, if unmarried, as a spinster would have had to care for her aging parents. Samantha's mother did marry at 30 years old, after her sisters had each taken their vows. She had given birth to a boy, Samantha's brother, and then the little girl herself, at the age of 32.

That was then, Samantha thought. This is now. The whole 'marriage' business is truly bizarre in different cultures, she decided, except strangely the same. She had just read in the newspaper, which she subscribed to on a regular basis, -"just to keep *au courant*", she said to herself - of a wedding in Tokyo where, in a lavish banquet hall, a 31 year old bride, dressed in a scalloped white gown, married her single self.

"I'm worth it," the bride declared. "I am empowered. I don't want children. I don't want to take care of older relatives. I saw my mother unhappy, with taking care of children and aging parents. She was worn out. And in older generations, husbands were the bosses of the family and the wives were obedient and weak. Not for me! I want to live a fulfilling single life. Therefore, I say 'I do... to ME!'"

"That's a new one," Samantha said with a smile to Abbi, who sat on her lap.

"Japanese women who remain unmarried after the age of 25 are often referred to as 'Christmas cake'," Samantha continued to read, this time aloud. "It was a nasty slur comparing the women to holiday sweets that cannot be sold after Dec. 25th."

"Because they go stale?" she asked of Abbi. "At 25 years old?" Samantha shook her head.

In another newspaper article, she read that 'pretty girls' in Singapore who were victims of sexual harassment, often faced shame and blame. The allegations cast a spotlight on the victim and her family, with the potential for dire consequences to her career. The public was skeptical of victims because there have been 'false accusations' of sexual harassment, a big problem, with the charge that the young woman was purposely lying.

"It's everywhere," Samantha said to Abbi. "Everything is now in the open air. I suppose it's for the best, but honestly, little dog, sometimes things go over the top." She scratched Abbi behind the ears.

"Listen to this," Samantha said, picking up her most recent copy of the paper and reading aloud: 'MISS AMERICA' is now considered a 'competition' not a 'pageant'. Swimsuits are out. The runway is gone. The contestants are now 'candidates'. Good lord. What next? Oh, look," she remarked. "Here's something about 'VICTORIA'S SECRETS' – they are going to use more 'demure' outfits in the company's fashion show – less salacious – and they're looking for transsexual models. Wow."

Samantha paused but then exclaimed, "And get this one, Abbi," and she read, again from the newspaper; "'Berkeley, California is to purge gender from its law books. For example: the word 'manhole' is now called 'maintenance hole': 'sisters and brothers' are referred to as 'siblings': he/she are banished in favor of they/them (even if only one person)".

Gender has no relevance in performance, the city of Berkeley's powers that be had evidently determined. 'The law applies to traffic, health and safety regulations, construction permits, all the business of the city, even garbage collection."

"Garbage collection, yet!" Samantha laughed. "That reminds me, Abbi. Donald Trump called Hillary Clinton and also Meghan Markle, each "a nasty woman". In colonial times, a "nasty" woman is one who refuses to remain in her proper place as defined by men, a female who challenges male authority. Trump also just called the Prime Minister of Denmark, Mette Frederiksen, a woman, "nasty" because his offer to buy Greenland from Denmark she had labeled "absurd".

"Ah, words. Words. Do they have meaning anymore?" this question aloud. Then, to herself, she added, And how about those words describing the ways of love! God help us. Nonbinary. Non-monogamy. Polyamory. Pansexuality, Bisexual. Transgender. Cisgender, which apparently means you are the sex you were born with?

It's one thing: Lesbian, Gay, Bisexual, Transgender – I understand their movement, to be free to love as they wish. That's more than fair – but all the other verbiage. Apparently, now they have added a Q to the list of letters – meaning 'questioning' and an I for 'intersex,' an A for 'asexual' and even a + sign for someone not included. So the list now reads: LGBTQIA+!

"It's mind-boggling. Hey. Maybe Mindboggling could be a movement too, do you think, Abbi?" Samantha declared, laughing out loud, as she removed the little dog from her lap, and headed to the bar for another vodka Perrier.

"It's enough to drive one to drink!"

THE FATHER

Marcie/Jake had stayed with Samantha for only five days on her visit from Los Angeles. It was enough for them both because, though affectionate with each other, there was a distinct tension between them. They did not discuss the 'situation' again, kept conversation to politics and Marcie/Jake's plans career-wise (movie-editing, "like my daddy" was 'their' ambition).

When Marcie (Samantha could not yet think of her as 'Jake'), had finally left the townhouse in Atlanta to return to California, her grandmother decided to call Matt Hayes on the phone. As Marcie/Jake's parent, he must have some response to this name-change, transgender transformation of his young daughter.

Samantha knew it would be a sensitive conversation to say the least – particularly on the telephone. She called Matt's office at the LA movie studio where he was employed as editor.

She had not wanted to speak to Maryelena, Marcie/Jake's mother, who Samantha had always found a bit hard-edged and difficult, although Matt seemed happy enough in the marriage.

Marcie – Maryanna – now Jake - was their only child.

Matt's cheerful voice answered the call. "Well, dear Sammy. It's so good to hear from you. Hope you're well," he exclaimed.

"I'm okay, Matt."

After a pause, he said. "I can guess why you're calling."

"I'm sure you can."

There was a silence, then a sigh from both, which brought a tender little laugh from each.

"She...he...they just left," Samantha said. Matt was silent, so Samantha continued. "I am quite stunned by the news," this said softly.

"I am too," was his response.

"I can't get my head around it. She... Jake... is so young to transition like that – it's irreversible..."

"I know. I know," Matt broke in. "Frankly, we're quite devastated, but she... Jake's our daught... our child and we love her... him, nonetheless."

"Of course. I do too."

"She... he... Jake told me they wanted to visit you – to tell you personally about all this, you know... she...Jake... has always loved you."

"It's mutual, you know, Matt. I've adored my granddaughter... um..."

There was silence again, a longer moment. Then, Samantha said, "Tell me, Matt. Were there signs of this... change? I mean earlier... when she – he - was hitting puberty, in high school?"

"No," he said flatly. "Nothing. In fact, Marcie was such a pretty, popular girl, she was a bit hard to handle. She had a lot of boy dates... appealed to many a young stud, believe me. That's why it's been such a shock."

"I'm sure. She was beautiful. She still is, in a boyish kind of way." Samantha paused, then "Did she ever explain why?"

"Never," was his reply. "We first noticed her becoming - well, reticent around us, oh, sometime last year. Then, she began cutting her hair – from the long tresses she was so proud of to a short bob and finally to a boy cut."

"Do you think she always wanted to be male?"

"God no. She was always such a girly-girl." Matt laughed. It relieved them both. Then, he continued seriously. "Now, she's gotten involved with this – oh, I don't know – bisexual woman and her Spanish boy friend they're all living together... and Marcie... Jake says she's in love with this Robin person."

"Have you met her?"

"No, but I did see her when I dropped Marc... Jake off at their apartment."

"And?" Samantha asked.

"Well, you could say this Robin is not my type. She's a big woman with long platinum hair. I didn't see the boy friend. Jake tells me they call the arrangement a 'V' whatever that means, but he - I'm supposed to call him 'they' - the boy friend, are allowed to go out and date other women."

Samantha was quiet. Then, she said, "And I know Marcie wants a baby. Now, as Jake, it will be Robin carrying a child because Jake will no longer have the equipment for it."

Matt chuckled. "I don't know why I find that amusing. Maryelena and will never have a grandchild for real – although maybe the surrogate child of Robin and this Pablo. Oh, God."

"Jake told me that there will be three parents for the little baby and how great for 'it' to have them all fussing over 'it' and how they can share the chores."

"Yeah, I'll just bet Pablo will love to do diaper duty," Matt chimed in, and they both laughed.

"Oh, and also, how now there will be three sets of wages to pay for 'it'," Samantha said.

"Again, I'll bet Pablo may make excuses on support, believe me. Don't mean to be cynical, but that fellow has got it made – with two – one bisexual woman and one trans to take care of him."

There was another pause. "I'll let you go, Matt. I had to speak with you about this. I hope it didn't upset you."

"No, no, of course not. I always love talking to you. Hey, Sammy, I wonder what old grandpa Steven, would make of this Jake business. He was so proud of little Marcie.""

Samantha laughed. "He'd probably make a bet that the 'V' arrangement wouldn't last!"

"He'd probably be right!" was Matt's response.

"He usually was," she answered. With a final chuckle, they each rang off.

JUST IN TIME

STEVEN — Spring, 1962

Another blind date, Samantha asked herself? Who am I kidding? But she decided to go along with the suggested meeting, as her friend, Nancy Smythe, her boss at work at the advertising agency, was so sure about this man.

"Sam, wait 'til you meet Steven Hayes. I just know you're going to marry him!"

"Oh, for heaven's sake. Don't be ridiculous. I'm not even looking for that in the first place. Please, Nancy. It's absurd."

"You mark my words," Nancy muttered, but determined, planned an evening, in spite of Samantha's protests.

On the day of the projected blind double dinner date with Steven Hayes, Nancy, and her then boyfriend, Jack Francisco, a much younger man who worked for an Italian food importer, Nancy called and said that Jack had to go on business to Washington, DC and they had to cancel. "Too bad. We'll do it soon, I promise."

"Fine," was Samantha's reaction. In fact, she was kind of relieved.

The phone rang again. It was a male voice. "Hi, Samantha. This is Steven."

"THE Steven?"

He laughed. "Yes. THE Steven. Say, who needs Nancy and Jack? Why don't we meet at least for a drink anyway? I really would like to meet you... heard nice things."

"Oh. I don't know..."

"Come on. How can I persuade you?"

He certainly sounded charming, she thought. "Well, Okay. How will I recognize you?"

"I'll be wearing a Racquet Club tie."

"What does that look like?"

"It's red and blue striped." There was a pause. "Let's meet at the bar in the Essex House. Is that acceptable?"

"Yes. Yes, I guess so. What time?"

"6:00. I'll see you then."

"With your Racquet Club tie on."

"Right around my neck," and he laughed again, then, hung up.

What am I doing? Samantha thought to herself. But she had been struck by the sound of his voice and his genuine laugh. It was deep and somehow penetrating. Her next thought was, what'll I wear, always a good sign, and she realized that she was actually quite excited.

"A red and blue striped tie, eh? I guess I'll go in black and white." With that she went to her closet and found a stunning V-necked black silk dress, (designed by Norman Norell, Anne Green's employer), and a white linen coat.

Samantha had heard of Steven Hayes. He was a political reporter for The New York Herald Tribune. In fact, she had read some of his articles and found his words often amusing enough for her to laugh out loud. He certainly was bright and pretty astute when it came to politics. And besides, Nancy Smythe was obviously impressed.

"Let's hope," Samantha said to herself as she prepared for the cocktail date.

She took a cab at 5:30 to go to the Essex House. She didn't want to be late and wouldn't mind waiting patiently if he happened to arrive after she did. She felt she had done the best she could, appearance-wise, with a new rosy lipstick and a splash of Chanel#5. Ah well, Samantha thought, as she sat back in the taxi as it roared downtown on a truly dulcet early April evening.

The entrance to the bar at The Essex House was through a small hallway, and as she made her way, she saw a man coming from the bar, toward her. He had on a striped tie. She paused, gathering her white coat about her.

"Steven?" she asked in a quiet voice.

"No. My name is Bob, but, young lady, why don't you join me for a drink?" and he turned back towards the bar and offered her his arm.

"Oh," she fumbled. "I'm sorry. I expect to meet another gentleman, but thanks anyway," and passing by the extended arm, she proceeded toward the doorway of the bar, leaving 'Bob' immobilized and not a little angry.

Samantha saw Steven immediately. He was sitting at a small table next to the bar itself, and he rose to greet her as she came in. "Samantha?" he said with a grin.

She nodded, at which he broke into a huge smile and, looking at her with admiration in his gaze, exclaimed, "This is for me?" which made her return the smile as warmly as his own.

They ordered drinks, for her a vodka martini with olive, for him Scotch on the rocks. She noticed that the man, 'Bob', had entered the room and was sitting on a stool directly next to the table where Steven and she sat.

The two, on their single blind date, were talking at once, exchanging items of interest about schools and past jobs and for her, Paris, for him, World War 11.

Steven had piloted a bomber plane over Monte Casino in Italy, blasting the Nazi enclave atop that mighty hill. When the war ended, this bomber-pilot would never go up in a plane again, the experience of the closeness of death had been so intense.

(In later years, Samantha and he would always travel by train.)

Samantha noticed that 'Bob' was listening to every word they said, even making facial expressions, shaking his head, smirking. Steven became aware of 'Bob' too.

Because the attraction was immediate and deep, this 'blind' date had taken on a meaning of its own. Steven told her how, when he arrived in the Essex House bar, he had approached a lady sitting at a corner table and said "Samantha?" at which she responded, "No, the name is Nicole, but sit right down, fella," and she patted the seat next to her.

And of course, Samantha told Steven about 'Bob', pointedly so that man could hear her every word. Finally, Steven said, "Let's get out of here," and rising to his feet, throwing some cash on the table, said to 'Bob', "Sorry fella. You're not invited," and the two swept out of the room.

It was on to dinner, which, though delicious, she barely touched, and dancing close in his arms, at The St. Regis Hotel Roof Garden, then kisses in the taxicab riding home, and more kisses on the stoop of her 80th Street townhouse.

He did not press her further, but insisted that they should definitely see one another again.

"And I mean definitely!" he declared.

"And soon," she whispered.

"You can bet on it," he remarked in his best gambling way (one of Steven's only flaws – as Samantha was to learn). And with a final embrace, he left her there. She watched his tall figure turn the corner on Park Avenue, where he turned and waved.

Samantha was smitten. Really smitten. (So was he).

It had been a perfect evening. She was glad he had not pushed for more, although she was seriously drawn to his presence. He exuded such masculinity, and that, combined with a sweet, empathetic nature, had captured her.

"There's time," she thought. "Oh God. There's time for everything," and mounting the inner staircase, she went happily into her third floor apartment bedroom and threw herself on the bed – white coat and all.

THE HAYES BOYS – SUMMER 1962

Matthew Hayes, called Matt, was just eight years old when Samantha met him. His younger brother, Bradley, called Brad, was only five. Their father, Steven Hayes, had married late and had both children in his mid 40s. He had lost his wife, Helen, to breast cancer, three years before he had met Samantha.

As a widower, Steven had the daunting job of raising his two little sons alone. The three lived on 56th Street near the East River of Manhattan, in a pleasant enough apartment that Steven had rented for over 10 years, their family home. He had a live-in housekeeper/baby sitter, a plump, motherly woman named Eena, who cared for the little male family.

Of course, there were several females eager to move in and take Eena's job, for Steven Hayes was an attractive, viable man with much to offer, but he was unmoved by their quite obvious wiles.

He enjoyed the attention of these ladies, but he had not fallen in love. He had loved his wife, but the mourning was over, although Helen would always remain a part of him and his boys. In fact, at 52 years old, he hadn't thought about love – until Samantha crossed his path in her white linen coat and radiant smile, and then, that was all he seemed to think about.

His usual evenings after work had been spent at The Racquet

Club, wearing the signature red and blue striped tie, where he played a three-handed bridge game called Towie, for high stakes. Steven did love the gaming table – backgammon, poker, and of course the track. To Aqueduct, the New York racetrack, he was a frequent visitor. And there was Belmont too.

The Racquet Club games were sometimes interrupted when the players decided to go to a brothel in a townhouse on 51st Street between Park and Madison Avenues. If a wife or girlfriend should phone the club to speak to one of the men, they were told that that person was in the gym and would call back shortly.

And the man would call back, on his return from 51st Street, an hour or so later, and then back to the game. Although Steven did not participate in this 'interruption,' (he had no need to, since he had plenty of women to choose from), he found he was spending less time at The Racquet Club and many more evenings with Samantha.

As spring moved into summer, Steven and Samantha would ride in a carriage drawn by a horse named Apple, through Central Park on a soft evening, often with the two little boys, who fed Apple bits of carrot, even doughnuts, and sugar cubes.

These were adorable outings, and Steven was moved by the way Samantha let the boys come to her. She was gentle with them and receptive, not fussing over them in an unreal way, as so many of the women he knew did.

First, they were shy. Samantha let them be. Then, they began to ask her questions, and she responded fully.

"Do you have a kid?" Matt asked. "No," she replied. "I always wanted one, but I wasn't that lucky."

"I didn't mean to make you sad," the boy said, noticing the downturn to her mouth.

"Oh, Matt. It's not you who make me sad. It's just the fact that… well, I can't have children." This was true. After the miscarriage, much of her inner equipment had to be removed.

"That's enough, Matt," Steven interjected.

"No, it's okay," Samantha said. "After all, it's the truth." With that, Matt reached toward her from his jump seat and hugged her.

As time went on, Steven and Samantha grew closer and closer, intimate and more intimate. Their time together, in the early evenings, included Matt and Brad, but once they were put to bed by Eena, the two could be lovers and explorers of their beloved city – in the fall, walking by the Hudson River, under golden-red leaves, dancing often at The St Regis Roof Garden, even skiing down Park Avenue during an early winter blizzard.

For that, the boys joined them, and there was a snowball fight and much laughing and tumbling in the snow, which was deep enough to have all the Avenues closed to traffic.

It was after nearly a year together that Steven asked Samantha to marry him. It was at the St. Regis Roof Garden. The song was "Just in Time." The drink was champagne.

The answer was "Yes."

LOVE

"Just in Time," he said. "That's you Samantha. That's what I believe. You arrived in my life like some sort of miracle."

Steven was close, next to her on the couch in her living room. He repeated the lyrics to the song, 'Just in Time,' in a sonorous voice.

"I wish I could sing the words to you, but believe me, I can't sing!" They both chuckled. "That was a lovely day…the Essex House evening…"

"And our interloper, 'Bob,'" Samantha whispered, which again drew soft laughter from each.

"Listen, lady," Steven said, sitting upright. "We have plans to make. You did say 'yes', didn't you? I did hear right, didn't I, over the St. Regis band?"

"You bet I did. And there's no going back," she said with a smile.

"Speaking of betting…"

"Oh, were we?" she said.

"You know I'm into it. I think I gamble because, in fact, my dad was an oil catter. He'd drill wildcat wells in areas not known to have oil. Sometimes, it would come in a bonanza. Sometimes not, so one year we'd have money, the next, not so much.

"So that's why," Samantha responded.

"I think so," he said. "Don't want to blame the old man but money was iffy at best. That's why I'm always looking for that bonanza."

"So, in our future life, should I keep my money separate?" Samantha was wary of this question, but she knew it had to be asked.

"Absolutely," he replied. "I make enough to support us – and the boys – and I keep aside a slush fund for my gambling projects," he said with a grin. "You keep yours for you."

"And for you and for them," she said, leaning forward and kissing him. This took several minutes.

"I'm looking for something in marriage that's drama-free," Steven said, sitting back with his arm around Samantha, gazing at the ceiling.

"You mean you're looking for a woman who never gets mad, who never worries about parents or money or her job? Hey, Steven, life is all about drama."

"I guess you're right," he said half-heartedly.

"Sure. It's important to face challenges together – even argue over them – roll with them. You know, being vulnerable and verbal makes for a better partnership."

"As long as we don't fight," he said.

"Oh, once in a while, a little fisticuffs are kind of fun," and she gave him a punch on his forearm, which brought him to roll next to her and begin to prepare her for love.

It was sublime.

Later, as she lay in his arms, Samantha could not help but worry. She thought of the Joseph years, of that man's infidelities that in the early days, she did not acknowledge. As time passed, she had not cared, but there was a humiliation that remained hidden inside her - Joseph's denigration of her womanhood. *Pierre* in her Paris days had done much to restore her sexual self, but Joseph, who had kept her away from friends and family, who had isolated her so she was his alone, had been unfaithful. Consistently. She could not go through it again. "Fidelity," she said softly.

"Fidelity what?" Steven asked.

Samantha sat up. "I demand it. Or no marriage," she said firmly.

"What?" Steven looked confused. "What's fidelity got to do with anything right now... just after all this," he said, with a sweeping gesture with his open palm over their two disheveled bodies. "I love you, Samantha. Didn't we just make love? Really make love?"

"Oh, darling, of course we did and it was perfect. But fidelity is all about this. It's just that I was burned in the past. I know I could never take the smell of another woman around you. I mean it. One suggestion of..." and she turned her face away.

"Hey. Hey," he said. "Look, my darling dear. For a man, it is a conscious decision, and one I can make easily, because it's you. You are the one for me... and the only one. Look, I'm 52. I want to spend the rest of my life with you, Samantha. I have believed you wanted the same."

"Oh, I do. I do. You know I do. But perhaps it's a conscious decision for a woman too."

"Really? Never thought of it that way," he said.

"Well, you'd better," she said with a laugh. "There are other men in this world."

"Is that a threat," he said grinning at her.

"No it's a promise. No other man for me."

As they tumbled together in each other's arms, he said, "Hey, was that our first fight?"

THE ONE

"Casablanca" was Steven Hayes favorite movie. He knew it by heart, word for word. So it became Samantha's favorite movie of all time too. In the early mornings, as she lay in bed alone for a few more blissful moments, Samantha would think of HIM. All her doubts and fears were cast away. He was the one and she knew it. Steven would be well on his way to work – "Hey, I'm a journalist and everyone has a story," he would exclaim on his way out the door.

It was so relaxed, so natural, the way it should be, her feelings. She wanted nothing back. There was no need to try. It was all there. He was all there. She loved the fact they were so open together, and that each was proud of the other.

Most of all, she loved the fact he smelled of typewriter ink and cigarette smoke (they both smoked); that, last summer, at the beach, his kiss was salty; how he looked with the snow falling in his hair on Park Avenue; the sound of laughter in his voice; the touch of his hand - all the senses.

She knew she was home.

Fortunately, he did too, as they planned their marriage.

It was simple enough, the ceremony, with the boys, (of course), and Samantha wanted Nancy Smythe as Maid of Honor, and of course, Richard and Anne Green as witnesses. They decided on a Justice of the Peace at City Hall. They also determined to remain in the 80th Street apartment for the moment.

Samantha had introduced Steven Hayes to her parents over a dinner of veal Parmesan at the Italian restaurant, Il Gatopardo, in downtown New York. They were duly impressed. She informed them of the upcoming little ceremony – about which they showed extreme delight for they wished her to settle down.

"This time, you picked the right partner, it seems," her mother remarked. "We won't be there in person, but our hearts are with you. You know all we want is for you to be happy."

"Oh, Mom, never happier – and, as a bonus, I have two little boys now to love and raise. And Steven – it's his decency –and he's so vital – it's, I don't know, so refreshing."

"Well, that's a new way of putting it," her mother had responded with a little laugh. "Refreshing, eh?"

"Oh, you know what I mean. He's different and so full of humor."

"Now that is refreshing, and Samantha, we are there in spirit. All our wishes are with you two, and the little boys. Be sure to call us when the deed is done… when you can, of course."

A NEW HUSBAND

Samantha and Steven Hayes were married two days after Christmas in 1962. They had not known each for long, but the commitment, one to the other, was strong enough to make them rush to the Justice of the Peace at City Hall in Manhattan.

Matthew and Bradley accompanied them, with Eena in tow, and Nancy Smythe stood in as Maid of Honor, bringing with her a frozen Sara Lee orange cake for the newly-weds to take on the night train to Atlanta, Georgia, where they would spend a brief honeymoon. Richard and Anne Green were there to hug and kiss the bride and tell Steven he was "one lucky man" to have captured their friend, Samantha.

Samantha and Steven had been living at her 80th Street apartment, with the two boys in bunk beds in the guest room. He had given up the apartment lease on 56th Street. Although it was larger than Samantha's place, there was no way Steven wanted to live there again, with the ghost of Helen pervading the atmosphere. Not that Samantha would have minded, he thought, (she would have!) but the boys might be spooked by the memory of their mother.

It was crowded on 80th Street, but oh so loving. The youngsters were delighted with their sleeping arrangement, exchanging the top bunk with each other for a change of pace from time to time. Eena moved in while their now two parents (Samantha had applied for legal adoption of Matt and Brad) were away for a week in Southern comfort. After the brief marriage ceremony. Eena took the boys back to 80th Street. She was a godsend, available on any occasion.

The train ride to Atlanta, in a large compartment, was sexy and complete, with delicious moments in the dining car over breakfast - omelets, crisp bacon. In the evening, there was even a piano player in the bar, and Steven, (of course) requested "As Time Goes By." Samantha asked the young man to play "Just In Time."

They stayed at the Marriott Hotel northwest of downtown Atlanta on Windward Parkway in Alpharetta. It served elegant eggs benedict in the early morning in the huge double bedroom to the newlyweds, and downstairs, the main restaurant had a sumptuous buffet, or direct menu of fried chicken, southern style grits (loaded with cheese) and hot, crumbly biscuits.

"Man, this is southern comfort food for sure," Steven raved as he buttered a biscuit. "I could live here."

"You could?" Samantha was surprised. Both were such dedicated Manhattanites, yet Steven had been concerned about The Herald Tribune and his job. His newspaper was having major financial troubles. She knew he had already been in contact with The Turner Broadcasting System here in Atlanta about the possibility of working for them.

"Yes. I could." He paused. "How about you?"

"Well, I guess if you could, I could."

"Really?"

"Yes. Really." It had occurred to her at that very moment that leaving New York City might be the ideal way to start a life with her passionate new husband, free of the baggage of the past – for both of them.

"I understand the schools are pretty good," she said.

"And I love the skyline," he remarked with enthusiasm.

"Reminds you of New York?" she asked with a grin.

"No. It has its own style and grace. Quite stunning. Atlanta has its charms, for sure, and it's the fastest growing city in the country. Might be fun to be part of it. What say you, my darling?"

"I say the usual thing I say to you. Yes."

NOVEMBER 22, 1963

On Samantha and Steven Hayes return to New York, after their brief but oh so enjoyable honeymoon in Atlanta – "We're going to live here," she had remarked on one starry-lit evening, - they resided again on 80th Street, in the same tight conditions, knowing the living situation would change, and soon.

The boys were growing fast. They would need space for friends and Samantha and Steven could use more privacy and workspace – his typewriter and desk and file cabinet - took up part of the living room.

Atlanta, here we come, Samantha kept thinking to herself, fully aware of the fact that Steven had been talking with The Turner Broadcasting System and CNN in particular. A new life in a new city – no Racquet Club distraction and Aqueduct Racetrack to beckon her husband, she thought with a certain degree of satisfaction.

It was a little after noon when the phone rang. It was Steven. His voice was trembling.

"Sammy, turn on the TV."

"What?"

"Turn on the TV." His voice was stronger. "Kennedy's been shot!"

"Oh, God," Samantha cried out.

"I'll have to stay here for the next hours. I'll call you when I know I can get home – but, hey, are you okay?" Steven could hear her weeping.

"No… but, don't worry. I know you've got to get back to work. I love you, Steven."

"Darling, it's mutual. Talk soon." The phone went dead, as the TV came on live.

Samantha was mesmerized by the horrifying visuals on the screen before her. She sat alone, with a box of Kleenex in her lap and watched the rerun of the event itself, with Jackie, first trying to crawl out of the back of the open car, then cradling her husband's head.

There was the scene at the hospital, the final announcement of his death, even the moment on the plane returning to Washington, DC with Vice President Lyndon B. Johnson, taking the Oath of Office. Jackie stood beside him, stunned and silent, in her blood-spattered suit. Samantha watched it all – for hours – alone.

The boys were at a sleepover with best friends. Steven was still at The Herald Tribune, processing this horrendous news with colleagues, and Samantha was solitary in her grief.

This was the turning point.

A SOUTHERN LIFE

Steven and Samantha, with Matt and Brad, moved in September of 1964 to the townhouse in mid-Atlanta they had purchased and where Samantha lived to this day. On the first floor, there was a guest room, but upstairs a loft, a large space where they had a new bathroom built, placed a large TV in a corner of the room, added a couple of beds, a small refrigerator and the two young boys.

In the early 1960s, when The New York Herald Tribune had money problems and ad sales were low, before the New York office closed down in 1966, Steven had been deeply concerned. It was then that he approached The Turner Broadcasting System, and sought a job. In 1964, he was offered the position of CNN News Associate. Because of his background and expertise, his salary was generous. Eventually, he even did stints on camera.

"I guess I'm a pundit," he would tell Samantha with a chortle. "I've always looked down on 'punditry', but not any more. The pay's too good."

Samantha found a part time job at a Real Estate Office in Buckhead, the uptown section of Atlanta. She handled much of the advertising and went on photo shoots of properties for marketing purposes. It was a fine life they put together, Samantha and Steven, Matthew and Bradley. They even had a large yellow Lab named Charlie.

As they grew up, both Matt and Brad attended Emory University in downtown Atlanta, each graduating with a Bachelor of Arts degree and were off and running, Matt to Los Angeles with a film editing job, and Brad to the great Northwest, Seattle, where he found work on a newspaper as a cub reporter.

Life for the Hayes family was full.

For 23 years, Samantha and Steven were married. He died of a heart attack at the age of 75.

Steven was the love of her life. There would never be another. She had had the best. She knew it, and during the many days of grieving, she blessed the time they had together, the memories they shared, and the beloved boys, now young men, she came to believe were her very own.

Steven had been the fabric of her world, the most natural of lovers, and with such a free and humorous spirit, that loveable big male who loved her. Oh, they had their fights. They had travails over money, jobs, the kids.

But through it all, the commitment was strong enough to transcend any major uncomfortable wave, and they were, in all those years, able to fall in love all over again...just in time.

A FINAL NOW

OLD FRIENDS

In the spring of 1985, three months after the demise of Steven Hayes, Samantha had received a phone call from her old college friend Janet Moody. They had been in frequent touch over the years, but this particular conversation was in response to the obituary in the newspaper, about Steven Hayes death, that Janet had read.

"How're you doing, Sammy?"

"Not so good," was the reply. "I miss him so. We really had something..." and her voice drifted off.

"Can I come for a visit?" Janet asked. "Or is it too soon?"

"It's never too soon for you, Jan. Oh, please. Please come. You'd be doing me a favor."

"I'll be on my way in a day or two. Hang in there, Sammy. Maybe I can help you smile again."

"You always made me smile," Samantha said and found, for the first time in weeks, her lips had curved upward.

Janet had come and the memories shared by the two women brought more smiles, even laughs.

Samantha had been curled up on the sofa next to her dog, Abbi, and Janet, nursing a gin and tonic, sat in an easy chair next to them. "I hate to leave tomorrow – back to Texas and my now solitary life." (She had just gotten her second divorce.) "But I hope to come back and I hope I've cheered you a little."

"Oh, of course you have and come back tomorrow or don't go at all."

"I have to go. Business stuff… all the dirty little ends of a divorce." Janet rose and went over to Samantha and kissed her cheek. "But I'll be back."

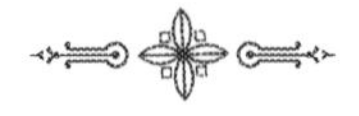

It was a long time before Janet Moody returned. She had an illness that impeded her movements for some years. She had a third marriage, brief, because her husband died in an automobile accident. Although she and Samantha were in touch often, by phone and email, Janet finally arrived in Atlanta for another convivial and rewarding visit with her dearest friend in October of 2019.

"We're both getting really up there," Samantha said with a grin, greeting Janet at her door.

The two embraced as the driver who had brought Janet from the airport, removed her one suitcase from the trunk of his car. Janet was walking with a cane, but her smile was infectious, her voice strong, as she said to Samantha, "Yeah. Really up there! We're two hot messes, right?"

Their embrace in the driveway was filled with genuine humor and love.

It was as if no time had passed, since they had seen each other, yet here they were, well into the new century. It was early fall and still Georgia hot.

As usual, over their drinks in the evening, while dinner - a stew was in the oven, or a cold supper of shrimp salad and avocadoes awaited in the refrigerator - the discussion between the two women always turned to the state of love in today's world.

"We've both had our fill of romance," Janet was saying, "although each so different."

"For me, Joseph was one kind of man – domineering, tough, even quite cruel… and he was hardly trustworthy."

"That's putting it mildly," Janet said. You know, he never really saw you – who you were… are, Sammy."

Samantha paused. Then, "My Steven was a prince."

"I know. With Steven, you hit the jackpot. But that's enough of them." Janet could see the mention of Steven's name brought sadness to

Samantha. "Today, things are so different," Janet said quickly. "When we were in college, what seems a thousand years ago, if you went with a guy, you were considered 'fast', 'cheap'."

"Today, if you don't go with a guy, you are considered 'a dork'," Samantha said.

"That's not all," Janet continued. "One hears such awful accounts of sexual assault, in which consent is disputed – often the girl victim accused of provoking the attack – and have you read about the toxic swirl of partying and hook-up culture, especially on college campuses that goes on today? It's quite shocking."

"I have indeed. Hey. Do you know the story of the young man of 'privilege' who raped an intoxicated 16-year old girl at a party, made a cellphone video and shared it with friends, adding: "When your first time having sex is rape."

"God, no," Janet exclaimed.

"The boy's mother decided his life would be devastated if a charge of rape against him was made. 'He's from a good family, in an excellent school where he is doing extremely well and an Eagle Scout,' that mother wailed. Can you imagine?"

"No, I can't imagine."

"And it gets worse. The Judge – yet – mind you, the Judge - pronounced the boy was a candidate for not just college but a 'good college'. He trivialized the harm to victims of sexual assault and focused instead on harm to the perp. In the 'he-said-she-said' world, the 'he' most often wins."

"Still! Has nothing changed?" Janet said with a sigh.

"Well, maybe somewhat. A backlash followed the news that a Judge had spared a 16-year old boy from being tried on rape charges as an adult because he 'comes from a good family'."

"Wow. Well, at least that's something," Janet said lifting her glass.

"It get's better. That Judge was forced to resign."

"That calls for another drink," Janet exclaimed.

"I'll get one for you and one for myself." Samantha rose and refilled their separate drinks. As she handed Janet her gin and tonic, she said, "You know, in spite of the terrific work that #MeToo does, there is a certain hypocrisy abroad."

"Thanks for this," Janet remarked, lifting her glass again to Samantha. "What do you mean, hypocrisy?"

"Well, frankly, some women are more predatory than men. The blatant sexual image that some women present is so hypocritical. 'You can all view me. You can all desire me, or desire to be like me. But you can't touch. I am pure, despite the fact I look like a beckoning lady of the evening.'"

Janet laughed.

"Naked up the kazoo," Samantha exclaimed. "Everything padded surgically - even the lips – with huge breasts and rear-ends like orangutans. Who are they kidding? Hey, did you know that now there is a garment, like a padded bra, only you wear it around your hips so your buttocks are enlarged? Talk about orangutans!"

With that, Janet burst into gales of laughter. "Orangutans! What an image. And you know, you're right. I remember when Marilyn Monroe's nude calendar was considered a scandal, but today, everything just hangs out for all to see."

"I read, last year, a defense lawyer in Ireland cited a 17-year-old's lacy underwear as a sign of consent to rape," Janet said.

"And get this, Janet," Samantha remarked. 'As long as there are many beautiful women, there will be more rape cases,' pronounced by one President Duterte of the Philippines. Now, there's another creepy male attitude..." Samantha was spluttering with anger.

"Yet, some men are quaking, partially because of the #MeToo movement," Janet remarked.

"Listen, as long as men have power over women, they're going to try to have sex with them. How about the hook up clubs where a man picks out a girl across the room, texts her, they go have sex, and he goes back to his buddies and boasts of the conquest, while she – or most shes – subside into a bleak despair."

"I know. And then he finds a second and maybe a third conquest to be racked up in the course of an evening. The bigger the number, the bigger the man! In his dreams." Janet put down her empty glass. "Hey, Kiddo, time I go to bed."

The evening was at an end.

MATT

Janet Moody was not Samantha's only visitor the fall of 2019. She was surprised when Matt Hayes called from California and told her he was arriving in Atlanta on a business trip the first of November. He had a reservation at the Marriott Hotel in Alpharetta and wanted to at least have dinner with her.

So she invited him *chez elle*.

He arrived on a cool evening, bringing a bottle of *Cabernet Sauvignon* to his stepmother in one hand and a bouquet of bright, yellow roses in the other.

"Ah, Matt, my dear," was Samantha's warm welcome and delight with her gifts.

The townhouse smelled of a leg of lamb in the oven (Matt's favorite), a small fire was going on the hearth, and as he opened the bottle of wine, he told her how well she looked.

"Considering," Samantha said playfully. They sat together on the sofa, wine glasses in hand, Abbi in her little bed in between.

"You look great," he said, as they clicked glasses.

"You're kind."

"I'm not being kind. I mean it."

There was a silence. Then they both spoke at once and the word from each was "Jake..." They paused. Finally, Samantha asked, "How is he doing?"

"I hate the word 'he'," Matt answered," but I do believe she... they feel they've found themselves. I'd say that Jake is relatively happy, but you never know, Jake really has a problem with Pablo."

"Jealousy – because of Robin? I know Jake kind of loves her, and the three, in the same house..."

"Probably. Who knows?" Matt was quiet as he sipped his wine. "I still want to call him Marcie."

"Ah, Matt." Changing the subject, Samantha asked, "and Brad? How's your younger brother doing?"

"Oh, you know Brad... never married. Of course, he's straight."

"You mean cisgender," Samantha interjected.

"Cis what?" Matt sat up.

"In today's language, cisgender means as you mature, you remain the same sex as what was on your birth certificate."

"Huh! That's a new one for me. Anyway, Brad's a bit of a runaround."

"Yes, he was something of a perennial Peter Pan," Samantha said with a smile.

"You can say that again. He likes woman who are not over 40."

Samantha snickered. "Good luck with that."

"Oh, he's had a couple of long term affairs with women, the latest terminated last year. He's dating again and tells me that it's weird out there."

"How so?"

"One recent sexual encounter, he thought he had to ask for verbal consent every step of the way."

"You're kidding."

"No, I'm not. Apparently, the woman chastised him for it, and told him, 'If I didn't want it, I would stop you.' This made him so uncertain. 'Was it wrong to ask the questions?' he asked me, of all people. He was legitimately confused. Then he told me, 'Now, I guess I'll just sit back and wait for the girl to make the first move. I don't want to overstep my boundaries.'"

"Well, of course, in the past, powerful men could force their desire on women whose silence they could count on," Samantha said. "And sometimes women would fake orgasms, giving a man an exaggerated view of his own – shall we say - talents?"

Matt chuckled. "We are getting pretty frank."

"Why not?" she responded. "But questioning every move! Is it ok to go to the bedroom? Is it ok to take this off? Is this ok?"

"Sounds unreal," Matt said, replenishing their wine.

"What if she asks HIM 'Is this ok?'" Samantha suggested."

"He'd probably say, 'I ask YOU that.'"

"'Why?'" she'd probably ask."

"Because he's the one who could make her do something she didn't want to do – not vice versa." Matt put his glass down. "And this #MeToo movement or whatever it is." He shook his head.

"#MeToo can backfire. Sometimes it goes too far. Some women get addicted to the victim role. But all we females really want is for men to listen."

"I hear you," he said with a smile. Then, "Overall, I guess #MeToo is a good thing," as Samantha rose.

"I smell that the lamb is done," she said and headed for the kitchen. "Want to carve?"

"You bet," was the eager answer.

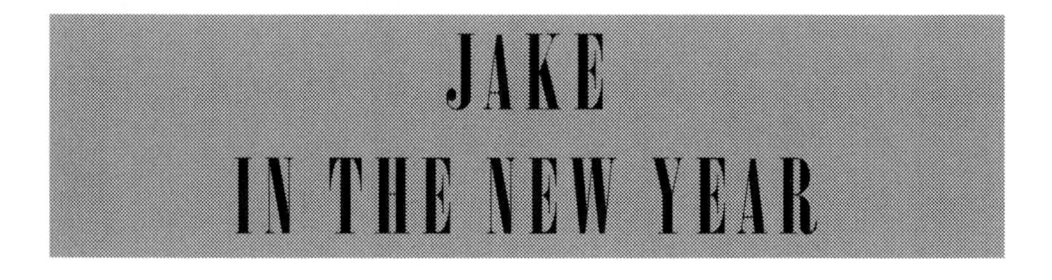

When Samantha's grand... Jake... arrived in Atlanta for an after Christmas visit, the older woman was struck by how different the appearance, after only a few months.

It was not only the clothes –shorts with tights underneath covering the legs, and heavy man-like shoes, but it was the body, and most of all the face. The dark hair was cut short and framed a pale brow, over thin cheekbones, however the broad smile was there, with even white teeth, and Samantha hugged this youthful person to her with all her might.

"Darling," she said.

"Ah, Grandma. I've missed you."

Samantha leaned back. The voice! Jake's voice was that of a young man.

Jake headed for the guest room, pulling a small bag, returning to the living room sofa where, on the coffee table, Samantha had prepared a sumptuous snack.

"It's close to 4:00 o'clock and a while before supper. Thought you might be hungry."

"Yes, I am!" Jake exclaimed, picking up a bread stick wrapped in salami. "Are those olives *Niçoise?*" Jake said grinning. "I adore them," placing several on one of the small napkins lying next to the platter.

"You want a Coca Cola?"

"I'll get it," and Jake practically ran to the refrigerator and retrieved the can.

"Get me one, too," Samantha called.

Jake returned with the two drinks, and settling beside Samantha on the couch, next to Abbi in her caramel colored bed, Jake sighed. "This is so great being here with you Grandma. I can't tell you how often I think of you."

"I miss you too, darling." Samantha took a sip of the cold Coca Cola. "How are things going for you, Jake?"

"Oh, I can't complain."

"You're still...?

"Yeah, still the same arrangement. I'm not crazy about Pablo – but Robin likes him, I guess, needs him. They're not pregnant yet."

Samantha put her can of Coca Cola on the coffee table, as Jake picked up a couple of the small cheese balls coated in chopped pistachios. "Let me ask you something."

"Anything, Grandma."

"Is pansexuality gleeful? Is the V situation a lot of fun?"

Jake looked quizzical.

"I guess I'm asking if you are happy?" she continued.

There was a long pause. "I don't quite know how to answer that, Grandma."

"I don't mean to pry, Jake," Samantha said slowly. "It's just that I remember at your age, I had such an excitement about life and love. I wanted to be adored by men. I began to feel the pressure of the 'male gaze'. Men, then, thought the ideal woman was gorgeous but not stuck-up about it; sexy but not slutty; ready for burgers and booze but still slender; eager for his lust, but she would never fulfill her own sexual desires with other men...oh, never, never, never."

Jake burst out laughing. "Times HAVE changed, Grandma, a lot!"

"Yes, I guess they have," and she joined his laughter.

"Grandma, now can I ask YOU something?"

She nodded.

"Are you a feminist?"

Samantha was surprised. "I'm uncomfortable with the label… what kind do you mean?"

"What kind of feminist?"

"Yes. There are lots of varieties…many forms – the militant kind, those ready to yell 'harassment' at the slightest infringement on their territory. That's not me."

"But you care about the #MeToo movement, don't you?"

"Yes, certainly. I think it's grand that women are demanding – and getting – more equality – in pay – in job levels – even a new balance in the bedroom."

"They're not all the way there," Jake interjected with a snort.

That's a Marcie remark, Samantha thought to herself, but she continued, "No certainly not, but in many ways, #MeToo has got the bad guys scared and that's a good thing. The minute they're not afraid anymore, they'd probably get worse."

"Not all men are bad," Jake said in a small voice.

"Of course not," Samantha responded. "But #MeToo demonstrates what American women are finally acknowledging what they have known all along – that sex is political."

"Political?"

"Yes, my dear. Political."

"How so?"

"Sex, for many men, is dominance. In other words, power - and power is a very political thing – or can be used in a very political way."

"I suppose so," Jake said, taking another salami stick.

"It's particularly true in regard to poor women and women of color. They are much more vulnerable to male assault and dehumanization. But don't think women can't be equally predatory, or even worse than the male counterpart."

"How so?"

"Oh, you must know how strong some women come on – and how provocative they can be in dress and manner. But, today, younger women feel heard, in a way that older women never were. And that's good. The #MeToo movement gives them that right. Us old ones, well we had to swallow the garbage... smile in the face of almost any affront or risk being called a shrew."

"You ARE a feminist," Jake said, rising. "I knew it."

"Well, I'm interested in fairness. I guess I'm an egalitarian – where equal means equal. I'm willing to work step by step toward a real equality. If that's what you mean in calling me a feminist, I guess I am one."

"You sure sound like the right kind," Jake pronounced firmly.

"I love you, sweetheart," Samantha said to her young trans. And she meant it. "Now let's have a real drink!" and the two, arm about each other's waists, walked over to the little bar.

I'M SO GLAD

It's surely a different world in 2019, Samantha thought. The Internet provides a new language. Sexuality does the same. It's hard for an older person to accommodate and understand, but it is the way of the world, the new world in which we live. In the digital space, it is passwords and pixels and icons and deletes and The Cloud, whatever and wherever that is. In sex, it is LGBTQIAT*

"Good lord," Samantha said out loud. "I'd like to add three more letters to that – LGBTQIAT* - OMG!"

She began to sing her little song, to a melody from somewhere in her past.

"A mind-boggling world is what I see,
And oh I'm so glad to still be me,
I would not change the many songs I've sung.
Oh I'm not sad,
Nor mad,
But glad
To not be young!"
Oh, yes!

AUTHOR'S THOUGHTS

The inspiration for SHADOW BOX comes from my realization, over the years of a long life, how drastically sexual mores and love relationships have evolved.

AND YET!

SEX, DECEIT, AND DOUBLE STANDARDS
A HEADLINE FROM 1894

(1893 was the year my mother was born.)

Madeline Pollard filed a Breach of Promise suit against Colonel W.C.P. Breckinridge from Kentucky.

Such suits were not uncommon in 1893.

Through a Victorian-era legal convention that recognized marriage as "a woman's primary vocation," a woman could recover damages for a broken engagement that left her "neither her virginity nor a wedding band to show for it." Madeline Pollard could have walked away from Breckinridge with her reputation intact, but, instead, she refused a settlement and sought a trial.

The Colonel and Madeline Pollard had met on a train – he 47 years old, and in his second marriage, she a 17-year-old student. They were together as lovers for nine years. The Colonel had repeatedly promised to marry her in the near future. Madeline Pollard had 2 children by the Colonel, who were put in a foundling hospital at his insistence –after which she had a miscarriage.

(The married artist, Picasso, was in his mid-40s too when he picked up Marie Thérèse Walter who was 17 years old, as she gazed into the window of the Gallerie LaFayette – in Paris in 1927, She became his muse for the next nine years and had a daughter, Maya, by the artist... an interesting parallel.)

Colonel Breckenridge broke his engagement to Pollard, after his wife died. Instead, he married a cousin.

In the South, well-to-do men felt free to sleep with slaves, servants and any other woman who came their way. Madeline Pollard was fair game and "utterly depraved where morality is concerned," the Colonel claimed during the trial. He assumed he had the right to seduce any woman who was not "a maiden" and "bore no responsibility."

In the end, the jury awarded Madeline Pollard a hefty sum and Colonel Breckenridge was ruined.

The case received an outpouring of public support for Pollard, in spite of the Colonel smearing her as a "wanton" and "experienced woman." Instead, he emerged as a bumbling hypocrite who promised marriage to two women. The suit was not about a ruined woman looking to even the score. It was about challenging the double standard that created ruined women in the first place.

Some say that the Pollard Breckenridge trial led to the start of the #MeToo movement.

What has changed in the 126 years since this trial took place?

Nothing and everything.

The sexual mores and love relationships still have similar bases, but today:

How much more public they have become. How much more blatant. How, often, much more vulgar do they appear. It is not just due to Internet access and the anonymity it provides. It is not just the speed with which information, dirt, and gossip travel.

It is the seeming separation of sex and love, which dehumanizes both.

The mystery of the dance of love is lost. Where is dear flirtation? Where is the game of love?

Undoubtedly there are true deep loves between people of all

persuasions. But there is a sense of gender confusion, partially caused by identifying it by a series of letters:

LGBTQIAT +

That seems cold and adds to an objectification of sexuality itself.

The #MeToo Movement is admirable in its reach for equality. It brings new power to women and some relief from the dominance of men in terms of harassment. Finally, the male can be exposed as predator in many cases of assault, for the first time, when, earlier, women have often borne guilt for the event.

The #MeToo movement has shifted the culture all over the world, but particularly in the courts. Women victims have gained power and authenticity.

In France, the movement is weaker. The French version of the #MeToo movement - *#Balance Ton Porc*– or #Expose your Pig –is not as strong as in the United States. "People want to see justice but they don't want to see names," is the cry. The French pride themselves on appreciating the art of seduction and flirtation in a way Americans do not. They feel the #MeToo movement punishes men unfairly in the work place when "they try to steal a kiss, or talk about intimate things during a work meal. One must understand the difference between flirting and going too far." How very French!

Women have sprung out of the shadow box, through the glass pane that has imprisoned them. The shadow box is now broken, glass spread upon the floor in shards, sharp pieces that can still cut and wound because the narcissism of male desire that powers men, is for them, still the ultimate aphrodisiac.

Printed in the United States
By Bookmasters